THE GHOST NETWORK

REBOOT

I. I. DAVIDSON

Andrews McMeel
PUBLISHING®

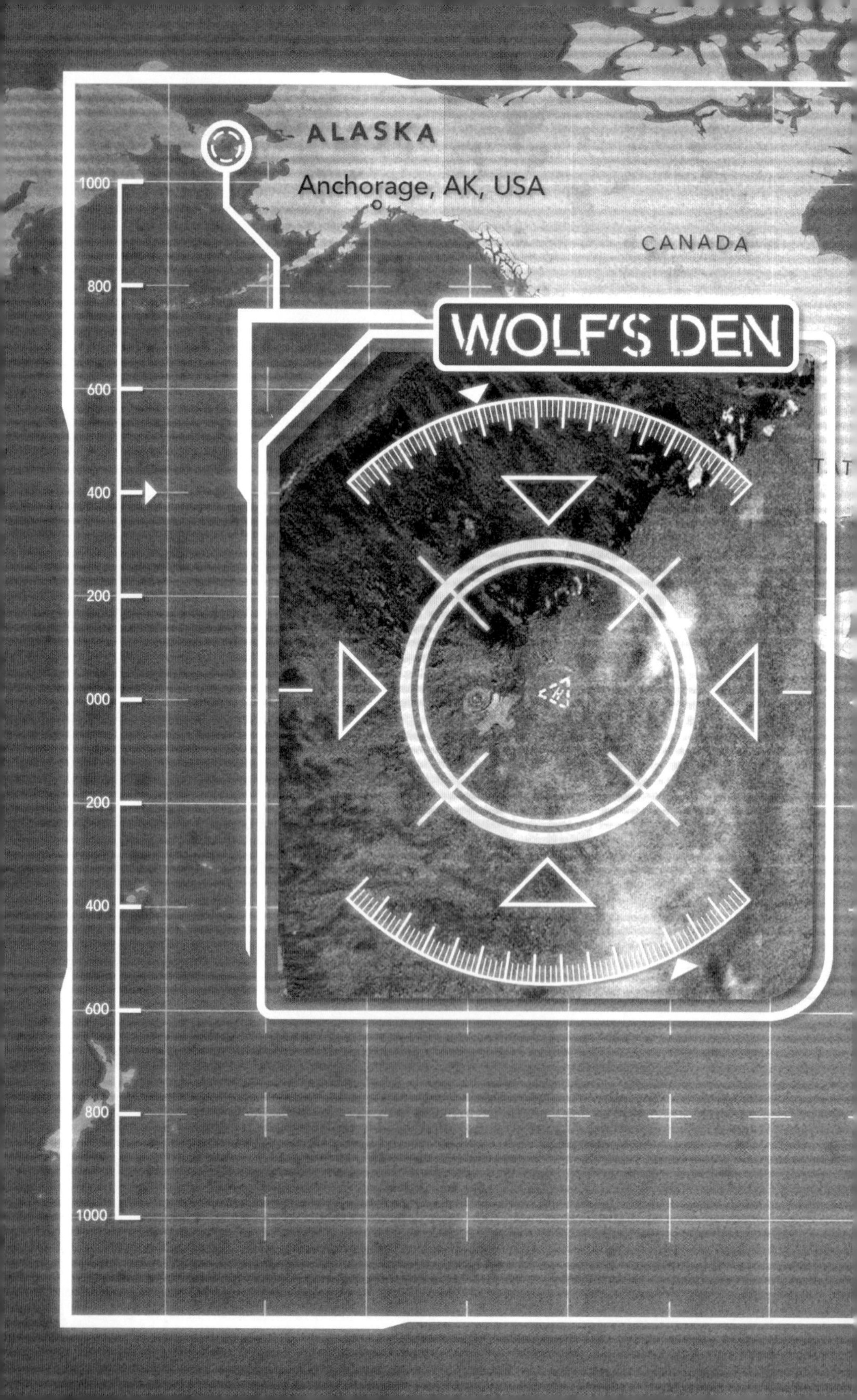
ALASKA
Anchorage, AK, USA
CANADA
WOLF'S DEN
1000
800
600
400
200
000
200
400
600
800
1000

MOROCCO
Casablanca o

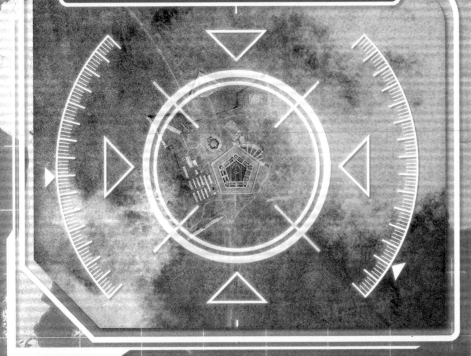

SCARAB'S TEMPLE

It wasn't what he'd expected.

The heat and the desert dust were bad enough, but Zhou Zhou had been looking forward to the air-conditioned splendor of a state-of-the-art complex. When his father had told Zhou about the Scarab's Temple, his voice was filled with excitement.

The facilities are out of this world, Zhou! Laine's centers are famous for it. Every technological wonder you can imagine—and then some! You'll have the opportunity to learn and study in a superluxurious environment but be careful not to let it distract you! All of your life I have dreamed about the day that you will graduate from this school. Work hard, my son. Here you will fulfill all your dreams!

All my dreams? wondered Zhou. *Or all of his father's?*

It didn't matter, though. 'Cause if this school turned out to be all that he'd been told it was, then the perks his father had described were unimportant. Zhou gave such a slight shrug that Marguerite Lagarde didn't even notice.

"And along this passageway you'll find the dining hall," she was saying in her businesslike tone. The Frenchwoman had not

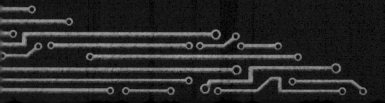

grown any more relaxed or friendly since Zhou had stepped out of the jeep and dusted the sand from his clothes. Even her welcome smile had been as tight and formal as the braided bun of her pulled-back hair; Zhou thought she seemed nervous.

"Meals are served at set hours," she went on. "You'll find the schedule in your room. Speaking of which, I will show it to you now."

Turning on her heels, Marguerite strode down another dingy corridor. The click of her heels was muted by the film of gritty dust that seemed to cover everything. Zhou followed, his expressionless eyes scanning the chipped plaster walls. A scurrying shadow caught his attention, darting from a crack between the floor and the wall.

"Your room is right he—*eeeeh!*" Yelping, Marguerite jumped away from the scorpion, her composure shattered.

Zhou stared down at the tiny creature. It froze for an instant, its tail curling up defensively, before it skittered back into another gap in the plaster. The only sound came from Marguerite's rapid breathing as she fidgeted with her collar and tried to regain her dignity. Zhou didn't say a thing.

"Yes, I—" Marguerite cleared her throat. "I—this is your room. Here." She jammed a plain Yale key into the lock and shoved the door open.

Zhou walked ahead of her into the room as she held the door. He stopped and gazed around.

Well. It seemed clean enough. His luggage had already arrived; it was stacked on the rug in the center of the room. Dust particles danced in the rays of sunlight that pierced the shuttered window and glowed on the plain concrete walls. In the far corner

<7>

stood an iron-framed bed made up neatly with white sheets and a gray blanket; opposite it, a sink was fixed to the wall. One of the faucets dripped. Someone had gone to the minor trouble of hanging a couple of pictures: black-and-white photographs of desert explorers who grinned at the camera, their long-suffering camels, horses, and manservants immortalized in the out-of-focus middle distance.

"Of course you're welcome to put up your own pictures. Your own things," Marguerite explained as she glanced around. "All the rooms are quite basic. I know the brochure is a little misleading at the moment. We're quite new, here at the Scarab's Temple. There have been, uh . . . problems with transferring funds from headquarters. We'll be bringing the facilities up to par with our sister operations around the world, hopefully very soon. But for now, I'm afraid, you'll just have to make do."

Zhou gave a single nod. It was obvious his silence flustered her. Good.

"You must have been expecting luxury facilities," she said, almost defiantly. "You're probably familiar with our other centers, of course. I expect you've googled them all—or sorry, is it Baidu that you use—?"

"Google," said Zhou calmly. "I can find my way onto any search engine I like."

"Oh. Of course. Well, whichever you use, you'll have seen them." Marguerite took a deep breath. She must have been unaccustomed to coldness like his because she suddenly made an effort to be chattier. "The Ma'yaarr Treetop Complex in the Amazon rainforest . . . the Weisshorn Alpine lodge, I know that's especially beautiful in the snow . . . the Wolf's Den on an island

<8>

off Alaska—it's concealed underground, you know . . ." Marguerite's voice had grown quite wistful, as if she dreamed of being posted somewhere far from this bleak warehouse of a school in the Sahara desert. Zhou couldn't blame her.

"Well." She shook herself, as if waking from a trance. "I'll leave you to get settled in. Make yourself comfortable, Zhou, and I'll see you again at the induction meeting."

He had opened his mouth to say a polite farewell, but he closed it again. A tiny red light caught his eye, blinking in the top corner of the ceiling. Tilting his head, Zhou stared up at the camera that watched him, small, black, and sleek. It looked like the most advanced technology in the whole place.

Finally silenced, perhaps by guilt or embarrassment, Marguerite said nothing as Zhou stared up at it. She was watching him, but Zhou ignored her, focusing all his attention on that gleaming lens. He studied it, taking his time to picture every wire within it, every connection, every circuit board, every sensor.

"Zhou . . . Zhou? Are you—" Marguerite stopped and gave a small gasp.

Smoke slowly started to trickle from the lens fitting, at first scant and pale, but quickly billowing into a darkening cloud. Zhou smiled. Yes, he had it now. With a sharp, snapping *pop* and a burst of white and yellow flame, the camera exploded.

He heard Marguerite's piercing scream, then the rapid tap of her heels as she ran out of the room, but he took no notice. Cocking his head to the side, he smiled up at the smoldering wreckage.

Marguerite returned within a few seconds with a security guard at her side. He had the darkest skin Zhou had ever seen,

<9>

and he was so tall he had to duck slightly to pass through the doorway.

"Look—it's ruined!" Marguerite pointed up at the burned camera. "Can you report it, Salif, and get it replaced? The electricity must have short-circuited again." Her voice shook slightly. She hesitated and turned to Zhou.

He turned to meet her gaze at last.

"Zhou? Did you have anything to do with . . ." She shook her head. "No. Sorry. My imagination's been on overdrive since I got here." All the same, her eyes were nervously suspicious.

Zhou made no comment; he just smirked. "I'll settle in now. Thank you for showing me to my room."

Marguerite and Salif exchanged a glance, but they didn't say another word. At least, not until they'd turned in the heavy silence and left the room. Perhaps they thought they were talking quietly behind his back, but Zhou could hear them perfectly clearly, even after Marguerite softly closed the door.

"Keep an eye on that one, Salif." Her whisper might as well have been a shout. "I think he's dangerous."

"Aren't they all?" The security guard said in a rough-edged, sonorous voice.

"Maybe." Marguerite's footsteps faded down the corridor as her voice grew fainter. "But this one especially, Salif."

Reaching out just in front of him, Zhou drew his backpack toward him and unzipped it. With a smile still on his face, he pulled out his PlayStation Portable.

You have no idea, Marguerite, he thought. *No idea at all.*

<10>

One

"Whoa! Tight corner ahead!" Slack's screech of warning also contained an air of excitement. Beside him, Salome wrenched the wheel, and the Tesla skidded sideways on the ice.

John Laine, leaning forward in the back seat, couldn't help feeling that Slack was enjoying this crazy ride a little too much. He held his breath until the Roadster's tires found traction on the slick road and shot forward again.

"Have we lost them?" Akane struggled back upright and turned to peer out of the narrow back window.

"Not exactly," said Salome grimly, with a glance in the rearview mirror. "Hang on. I'm going to disable the speed-limiting device."

John turned with Akane to watch their pursuers. The Tesla was the faster car, but whoever was driving that Mercedes must have been desperate not to lose them. It hurtled around the corner after them; John could just make out the intent, angry expressions of the driver and his passenger.

"Are you sure those goons can't regain control of the programming?" John asked. "Akane, do you feel any hacking attempts?"

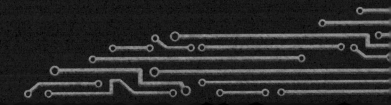

"No way." Akane shook her head just as Salome did. "These aren't Roy Lykos's people, after all. They're just security gorillas. They don't know whom they're dealing with." She grinned.

"Yeah," said Salome, her eyes still fixed on the road ahead. "They can't take control back from me. It's this ice that'll destroy us, if you don't stop *distracting me.*"

John rolled his eyes at Akane. "I told you all: taking this job was a bad idea."

"So did I," chimed in Salome from the front.

"Bad idea or not, we had to do it!" Akane looked indignant. "Carl di Lucci has been drilling in the North Canadian tar fields; you know that! Those fields are *protected.* Lucci Corp has no right to explore there!"

"Yeah, but who gave us this mission?" John was entirely on Akane's side where the tar fields were concerned, but he still felt uneasy. The Ghost Network's orders had come from a contact who had refused to reveal his name. If he hadn't used their own programming to infiltrate their heads as well as their phones, the four of them would never have trusted him enough to agree. And, even then, it had been a close decision. If Salome hadn't reluctantly changed her vote at the very end of the raucous argument, the four of them wouldn't now be hurtling down the frozen highway out of Anchorage with a stolen briefcase full of stolen documents locked in the trunk of their stolen car. John shook his head and sighed.

"Who cares whom the orders came from?" yelled Slack over his shoulder. "And to be honest, who cares about the oil company? We do this and we get more information! About our pasts *and* our future! Mystery Man promised us that."

<12>

"And, come on, John." Akane grabbed his arm in excitement. "This is *fun*."

He grinned. "I've got to admit I was getting kinda bored in California."

"John," scolded Slack, mock horrified, "nobody can be bored in California! And Salome's godmother is lovely."

"To be fair," pointed out Salome with a swift glance in the mirror, "Aunt Marjani *is* lovely, but let's face it: I could think of more exciting spots to spend a month than Sausalito."

"At least Marjani didn't ask any awkward questions about why we weren't at school." Slack yanked his hair free of John's white-knuckled fingers. "And John's mom thinks we're still at the Wolf's Den."

"Hah! I'm just glad Tina doesn't understand tech," said John, slumping back.

Tina Laine had been completely convinced by their live-action animation of Roy Lykos, the creation that had Skyped her when the four of them had reached Sausalito. Calling John's cell phone afterward, she'd even exclaimed that Roy seemed like *such* a nice guy.

If only Mom knew, thought John grimly. *But I guess it's better that she doesn't.*

"You think it was your dad who gave us this mission?" Slack leaned over the seat again. "He did say he'd contact us when we were safely in Anchorage."

"Maybe." John shrugged. He hadn't actually dared to hope. He'd spent so long accepting that his father was dead that he still found it hard to believe that Mikael was alive and well—and looking after his young "Ghosts" from afar. That Mikael had

<13>

actually "created" all of them, rebuilt their brains with advanced AI technology when they were each on the brink of death . . .

"I know I said don't distract me," snapped Salome, her white knuckles grasping the wheel. "But it'd be nice if you all didn't just chat among yourselves and let me do it on my own!"

"Sorry!" John touched her shoulder apologetically. At that moment she swerved again with a yelp, letting the Tesla arc into a three-hundred-and-sixty-degree spin on a broad patch of black ice. Akane collided with John again, and Slack's head bumped hard off Salome's shoulder; then the car corrected itself again under Salome's skillful hands.

"That's it." She punched the touchscreen. "I disabled the limiter. Yes!" As she depressed the accelerator, the Tesla shot down a side road and onto another highway—

"We're hitting the Glenn Highway!" shouted John as a blurred sign flashed before his eyes.

Slack clutched the dashboard as he blinked at the speedometer. "At two hundred and twenty miles an hour!" he yelped.

Salome veered into the left lane and overtook a line of cars; she stayed there, since it wasn't worth slotting back into the inside lane. They were traveling considerably faster than any other vehicle. She glanced calmly in the rearview.

"We're going to lose them," Salome confirmed, cool and satisfied. "Easily."

"Awesome," said Slack. For all his whooping bravado, there was an edge of distinct terror in his voice. "Though maybe we could just have taken a cab . . ."

<14>

Two

Taking a cab had not been an option, and Slack knew it as well as any of them. It had been a pure stroke of luck, thought John, that they'd spotted Carl di Lucci striding across the parking garage at the Ted Stevens International Airport in Anchorage. The sleek red Tesla had been too distinctive to miss, and it had taken them just minutes to hack their way into the Roadster and access full control of its computerized systems. It was just a shame that Alaskan state police were faster to respond than they might have thought—they'd been pursued before they'd even made it out onto the airport's highway exit.

"Tell you what," said John with a slow grin. "Even if we end up in jail, this was worth it for the look on di Lucci's face as we passed him in the parking garage."

"We're not going to end up in jail." With another glance in the rearview, Salome eased her pressure on the accelerator, and the car slowed to a mere 100 mph. "We lost them miles back."

"What about that briefcase?" John asked. "We can't abandon the car till we can get it out of the trunk."

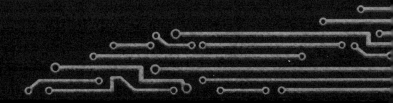

Salome frowned. "Di Lucci's obviously had the trunk converted into some kind of locked safe. Now's as good a time as any to try to break in. John, Akane—can you get through from this side?"

There wasn't a lot of space in the Roadster's rear seats, but John and Akane wriggled around and peered together at a small touchscreen panel.

"Yup," said Akane. "This is a special feature. It's got to access the trunk. I don't know what else it would be for."

Blowing the scarlet fringe of hair out of her eyes, she shook herself briefly and closed her eyes. *She's thinking her way into the system*, realized John. He'd done it himself before, without even knowing what he was doing, but Akane had a special aptitude for it; maybe it was her experience in meditation or simply the intense focus she'd learned while trying to avoid dying in BASE jumps and dangerous parkour stunts. He watched a profound expression of peace settle on his friend's face; she didn't seem affected at all by the speed of the car. Behind that calm mask, John knew, calculations were being made and pathways decoded at a breakneck rate that would put a Tesla Roadster to shame.

"How's it going?" Salome called back over her shoulder. "I got the speed fixed quicker than this."

"Just give me another few . . . *ah!*" Akane jerked back as she touched the screen and a concealed panel slid back. "We've done it! There's the briefcase!"

John lunged eagerly forward into the dark space beyond—

And it suddenly wasn't a dark space. As he leaned forward, he brushed Akane's arm, and she hit the control pad once more. A blast of air rushed through the trunk as the outside lid popped

<16>

open. At the same moment, Salome, distracted, swerved the car onto the shoulder, then twisted it awkwardly back on course. And just as John's fingertips brushed its handle, the briefcase jolted and shot out of the trunk.

They didn't even hear it hit the highway; the Mack truck they'd just overtaken had already thundered over the briefcase. It vanished between the wheels, and John swore with passion.

"Stop! We lost it!"

"I can't! Look at this traffic!" Salome was slowing, but the truck was too close for sharp braking, even at this speed.

"We've got to!" yelled Slack. "If we lose those documents, this whole escapade was all for nothing!"

"*Fine!*" Salome yanked the brake sending the car into a hundred-and-eighty-degree turn. They all screamed at once, as the car slid with a squeal of rubber onto the shoulder. They were all violently flung forward against their seat belts.

"How are we going to get it?" yelled Salome.

Akane sucked in a breath. "I blew it—I'll do it." She was out of the car before anyone could protest. With his heart in his mouth, John looked back to watch her, already running hard back down the highway shoulder.

This time it was Salome who swore. Turning back around, John noticed that Salome wasn't watching Akane. Her horrified stare was fixed on the rearview mirror, and now John, too, heard a familiar wailing noise.

"The cops!" yelped Salome.

John could see the blue and red flash of lights, perhaps a mile back but drawing swiftly closer as cars pulled over to make room.

"She's got about twenty seconds," breathed Slack.

<17>

Come on, Akane! Run! John found himself clenching his fists as he watched her small figure pause briefly on the edge of the road. Then she darted out and flung herself toward a barely visible dark object in the roadway.

"Akane!" he yelled, though there was no way she could possibly hear him. Another huge Mack truck was bearing down fast on the girl, its horn blaring.

John barely caught her rapid movement. Akane pivoted and leaped, and as the truck thundered past, she kicked against its side with both feet, launching herself farther into the roadway. Snatching the briefcase as she ran, she sprang for the center median.

"Don't make her cross the road again!" gasped John. The way she channeled her AI was awesome, but there was no point overloading it. "Drive, Salome!"

Salome pulled sharply back into traffic, which garnered a fierce return of angry honking. The blue and red lights were close now; the flashing of them seemed to fill the entire car. John could hardly bear to watch as Akane sprinted back toward the Tesla, the briefcase clutched in her arms. A lot of cars were backing up behind them now, their drivers yelling soundlessly and gesturing, but Salome took no notice. Her face impassive, she slapped the touchscreen control on the dashboard, and the glass roof slid open.

"Come *on!*" screamed John, rising to stick his head through the open roof.

Akane barely adjusted her stride. Closing her eyes, letting her AI take over completely, she leaped into the air, bounced with one foot off the edge of the trunk, and hurtled inside through the

<18>

open roof. She smashed into John, and he grunted, winded at her impact. Then he felt the briefcase between them, digging into his ribs as Akane rasped a high-pitched squeal of belated terror.

"Go, Salome!"

Salome had already laid on the accelerator. In the sudden silence, Akane lay helpless and panting for breath on top of John, so he couldn't move anyway. He couldn't see anything beyond the leather of the front seats, and his seat belt felt as if it was about to slice him in half. However luckily, the flash of lights from behind them was dimming, and the sirens faded swiftly.

"That," said Slack with his usual talent for understatement, "was close."

Akane wriggled off John and shoved herself back into her own seat. Her face was still flushed, but she wore a triumphant grin. John, getting his breath back too, straightened up and high-fived her.

"We lost them again, but they'll be alerting other cars," said Salome firmly. "We need to lose this Tesla *now*."

No one protested. Exchanging glances, they all nodded; she was right.

Only Slack permitted himself a single, mournful whimper of remorse.

<19>

Three

"Slack still looks sad," remarked Akane with an edge of mockery as she strode on up the side of the highway.

"I can't help it." Dramatically, Slack flung the back of his wrist to his forehead. "That beautiful car deserved better."

The briefcase felt heavier by the second in John's grip. They'd been walking for miles now, but the glowing hotel sign was finally in sight. "The car won't come to any harm, Slack. We set it to driverless mode. It'll be way up west Parks Highway by now, and it'll find its way to that parking lot near Denali National Park. We programmed it perfectly. Don't you worry your pretty head."

"It deserved to be loved," moaned Slack. "It shouldn't be alone."

Salome giggled. She was usually so serious and intent that the very sound lifted John's spirits and he walked a little faster. Beside him, Akane kept pace; even in the dark, with her face buried in her phone, she was sure-footed and quick. *It's not just her AI; it's all that parkour,* thought John. *I bet she's never fallen over in her life.*

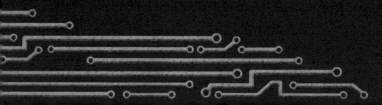

Well, except for that time she'd tried to fly from the roof of the Gotokuji Temple in Tokyo. She'd been only four years old then, and she would have died of her injuries without the intervention of John's father. All four of them had suffered similar accidents—and they'd all been saved by Mikael and his experimental AI genetic treatment.

Which is why we've ended up running from the cops with stolen documents, thought John wryly.

Akane gave a sudden laugh and looked up from her phone.

"The police have found the Tesla," she said. "It ran out of gas. Well, electricity. It's at a charging station just past Wasilla."

"Are you hacking the police computer?" asked Salome severely.

"Of course I am," Akane told her. "They're surrounding the Tesla right now, and they don't know what to make of it. All their guns pointed at an empty car."

"My poor baby," lamented Slack.

"I miss her too." Akane patted his arm as she winked at John. "But I'm sure they won't hurt her."

"And we're finally getting a bed for the night." John turned into the hotel parking lot and trudged toward the brightly lit glass door. Despite his aching muscles, he felt cheerful. "I think we can call this mission a success!"

"This mission is not a success till we get this briefcase open," declared Akane.

They were gathered around the shoved-together twin beds in John and Slack's room, with the briefcase perched on one of the

<21>

garish floral bedspreads. To John's fanciful eyes, the case looked downright defiant.

"To be fair," said John, "we were only supposed to retrieve the thing. There weren't any instructions to break into it."

"I won't consider it 'mission accomplished' till I get through those locks," insisted Akane. "No way am I letting this beat me."

Akane cursed and growled. "Why couldn't it be a digital lock? This guy di Lucci's a dinosaur."

"Guys," said Salome calmly. "The day I can't pick a lock—any lock—is the day I give up and go live in a yurt with a llama. You're overcomplicating this." She pulled the black leather case toward her and crouched till the lock was level with her scowling eyes. "Not everything's solved with tech." Her thumbs were busy at the combination locks, deftly spinning and clicking. "Sometimes all you need is a little experience and a bit of cunning and your *thumbs*—ah!"

She stepped back as the locks popped open. Slack gave a whoop of triumph, then clapped his hands over his mouth to muffle it.

"Honestly, Salome," said Akane, "one of these days I'll ask you how you learned to pick locks and crack safes."

"But today is not that day," drawled John, his excitement mounting. "Let's take a look at these documents."

Salome leaned forward and snatched up a bulky folder. Her eyes shone with excitement as she flipped it open and began to pass the pages to the others. "I want to know what was worth that whole escapade."

John grabbed the file she held out to him. "I take it that it all has to do with Lucci Corp's exploration of the tar fields."

<22>

Akane was already flipping through a ring-bound sheaf of papers and photographs. "It is." Her face looked pale; John knew she could speed-read like a rocket, and he frowned.

"What are you seeing?"

"I'll need to go through it all again more carefully, but I'm getting the gist of it." She stared up at him. "It's worse than we thought. They're planning to drill illegally in the Arctic."

"They can't do that!" exclaimed Salome.

"And they know it. There's pages in here about contacts with politicians, the leverage they have—blackmail and bribes—the legal loopholes they're going to use . . ." Akane brandished the file, an expression of disgust on her face.

Slack glanced up from his own reading. "The worse of it is there's a colony of Lacs des Loups Marins harbor seals right where they want to drill. They're incredibly rare." He jabbed a finger angrily at a sheet of graphs. "This project will wipe out the entire colony!"

They stared at one another. John felt a sense of helplessness rise inside him: *We're just four kids.*

"No," he said aloud, suddenly. "We're the Ghost Network. And we're not going to let this happen."

"Dang straight," said Salome with vehemence. "Roy Lykos might have originally intended us for sinister purposes, but *we're* in control now. And this seems like just the kind of thing we should be stopping."

"But how?" Slack spread his hands. "Where do we even start?"

"I suppose if our Mystery Man wanted this documentation, it means he's got plans to deal with it," suggested John, chewing on his lip. "Maybe we don't have to act till he gives us instructions?"

<23>

"I don't like that idea." Akane wrinkled her nose. "Who knows when they'll come after this briefcase? And I'm not waiting for some dull committee anyway. These drilling plans look well advanced, and we've got to do something *now!*"

"Wait." John froze, his knuckles whitening as he clutched the file.

"John?" Slack turned. "What is it?"

He couldn't answer. The sound in his head was like a barely discernable buzzing; he wasn't even sure whether it was a sound at all. Perhaps it was more of a . . . vibration? Whatever it was, it demanded his full focus. The room around him faded into a blur of dull color. All he could see was the image that appeared before his eyes: a clear, perfectly legible news webpage.

His eyes drifted to the byline—"by *Sentinel* Town Hall Correspondent **Sarah Lopez**"—then back to the headline. It seemed to bear no relation at all to anything he'd ever heard of.

"Municipal Crews to Strike Monday"

"Mayor Appeals for Dialogue"

John blinked, but the webpage stayed right in the center of his field of vision, vivid and clear.

"John? What's up?" Akane touched his arm. At the interruption, John shook himself and swept his arm across his face. The webpage vanished.

He blinked again, hard. "IIDA just got in touch with me again."

"In your head?" Slack was a bit startled, but also excited. John's best friend had been weirded out and a little angry the first time John had received telepathic instructions from the supercomputer that bound their network together. Nowadays, though, Slack was downright thrilled at any contact.

<24>

"Yeah. She showed me . . . um, the trouble is . . . I don't think it's relevant. Some local news story from a reporter called Sarah Lopez."

Salome set down the papers she was reading. "Sarah Lopez from the *Sentinel*? I know her!"

"You do?" John raised his eyebrows. Now it seemed like more than a coincidence.

"Sure. She did a story on the Center back when she worked for the *Western Gazette*. I showed her around. We got along great— we had some common interests. We still keep in touch."

"But the story didn't make sense. It wasn't relevant to us."

"Maybe not," said Salome, excitement rising in her voice. "But Sarah just might be. She's the environment correspondent now. She does a lot of investigative stuff about companies polluting, that sort of thing."

"IIDA wants us to contact her!" John could feel his own heart beating faster.

"Sarah would pick up this story and run with it in a heartbeat—I'm sure of it." Salome jumped off the bed. "I should have thought of her before; I'll message her right now!"

Having his head constantly open to IIDA took a lot of getting used to, thought John as Salome snapped photos and tapped urgently on her phone. He still felt uneasy about some supercomputer having 24-hour VIP access to his brain.

But he had to admit that it was an efficient weapon of choice for the good guys.

<25>

<<>>

"This is incredible!" Sarah Lopez was leafing through the documents, her eyes growing wider by the minute. Now and again she would scribble notes in a Moleskine, then peer in disbelief once more at the folders.

"I'm sorry you had to fly all the way up here," said Salome. "With no notice either."

"For heaven's sake, don't apologize." Sarah gave her a quick glance. "It's not like I could take your word and a couple of iPhone photos. I had to see it for real, because this is going to be my first huge scoop. And it really is *huge*. Lucci Corp is supposed to be too big to fail, but this is share-crashing stuff. There are going to be huge repercussions. But di Lucci deserves it, even if his employees don't."

The young journalist had dark pixie hair, and huge eyes dominated her very young-looking face. She wasn't much taller than any of the Ghosts—but John couldn't help feeling awed and a little intimidated by her. Sarah Lopez's expression was a combination of righteous determination and professional glee. She'd marched straight into their hotel room, dumped her overnight bag on the floor, and seized the briefcase's contents with barely an introduction.

She took a deep breath and looked up at last, scanning the Ghosts' faces. "But how did you guys get ahold of these documents? It's dynamite—I'm not kidding."

Slack opened his mouth to reply, but Salome interrupted him. "By accident," she said firmly, with a warning glare directed toward her friend.

<26>

"Some accident," said Sarah with a touch of skepticism, "but I'm not going to pry, because these look genuine to me. I'll have to have them checked, of course, and have the lawyers approve the story. But thank you. Seems like di Lucci was about to get away with this—if it wasn't for you meddling kids." She winked.

John grinned. Sarah suddenly looked a lot younger and more mischievous.

"I've got to get back to the office now. Give me forty-eight hours," said Sarah, shuffling the papers together. "The *Sentinel* gets the scoop, obviously. Soon as it's published, it's gonna be on every front page in the country."

The next couple of days were a maddening combination of anxiety and sheer boredom; the Ghosts didn't dare leave their hotel room, and they whiled away hours checking phones and refreshing Twitter. John was beginning to think they'd spend eternity in a hotel. When he woke on the second morning, he decided he wasn't even going to torment himself with CNN. Clicking on the room TV, he settled very deliberately on reruns of *Brooklyn Nine-Nine.*

Slack was already awake. Cross-legged on the bed next to John's, he was chewing lazily on a room service cheeseburger—*at this hour of the morning?*—but John almost jumped out of his skin when his friend gave a sudden whoop and tossed his phone into the air.

"It's up! Every major news site!" Slack shouted triumphantly, catching his phone. Reaching behind his bed, he banged on the

<27>

wall; in seconds Akane and Salome had run from next door to join them, blinking and still somewhat disheveled. "Look—the *New York Times* and the *Post. The Washington Post. Times* of London and India! And the British *Daily Mail*, check this out! And *Buzzfeed, Vice*—the lot! It's front-page headlines for all of them!"

"You're spilling your fries everywhere, Slack." But Akane was grinning, and she gave him an energetic fist-bump that made him wince.

"I hope our Mystery Controller intended for this to happen," said Salome, a little nervously.

"I'm not worried about him," drawled Slack. "IIDA clearly wanted it, and that's good enough for me."

"I reckon Mystery Man and IIDA are closely related, at the *very* least," said Akane firmly.

"I know who *is* going to be upset," grinned John, "and that's Carl di Lucci."

Salome laughed. "That can never be a bad thing."

A sharp double rap on the thin door quickly silenced their laughter. All four fell simultaneously quiet, and they stared at one another with wide eyes.

"Who's that?' whispered Slack.

"Dunno," John mouthed, shaking his head. His heart had lurched into rapid, pumping overdrive.

"You don't suppose the cops have found us?" Salome looked as if she was about to faint.

The knocking came again, more impatient this time. Abruptly, Akane shook her head.

<28>

"Whoever it is," she growled, "they're not going away." Straightening her spine, she marched to the door and flung it open.

She did it so violently that the desk clerk stepped back with an expression of startled shock. Then he cleared his throat and held out a trembling hand.

"Message came in for you," he said. "Guy said it was urgent."

"Thank you!" squeaked Akane and grabbed the message. She closed the door and brandished the thin brown envelope.

For a few long moments, they all stared at it.

"Who's going to open it?" asked Slack.

"It's not fat enough to be a bomb," said John. Taking a breath, he took the envelope and slit it open with his thumb.

Pulling out the single sheet of lined paper, he scanned it swiftly. Then he raised his eyes to his friends'.

"Well?" demanded Akane. "What does it say?"

John held the letter up so they could all see it. He could already recite the short message by heart.

"GHOST NETWORK: PLEASE REPORT TO THE TORTILLA GODZILLA RESTAURANT. IMMEDIATELY."

<29>

Four

What was it about cheap restaurant signs? It didn't
matter how garish they were, how brightly lit or cheerful, they
just looked sad. John eyed this one gloomily: it was attached to
the hotel on the north side. The four of them had to walk out of
the front door and cross the chilly parking lot to access it.

"MIGUEL'S TORTILLA GODZILLA!" read Slack, wrinkling
his nose as he stared up at the garish red-and-yellow lettering.
"What's with the exclamation point?"

"And how are you supposed to pronounce it?" asked Salome.
"Is that 'Tor-tiller God-ziller' or 'Tor-teeya God-zeeya'? This
Miguel can't have it both ways."

"I don't actually care," said Akane, rubbing her arms. "I'm
freezing, and it's the only restaurant, so for goodness' sake let's
get inside."

It was even more depressing inside than it was from the
outside. John slid past a giant plastic dinosaur—with a plastic
taco in its front claws—and led the way to a booth near the rear
windows. Fastidiously, Salome rubbed a wet wipe across the
cushion, then stared at it. None of them sat down.

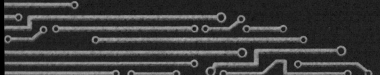

"It's *sticky*," said Akane, touching a fingertip to the table. "Give me that wipe."

"It's also tacky," remarked Slack. "Is this where plastic cactuses go to die?"

"Apparently it's where Mexican stereotypes go," said John, pointing a thumb at the man behind the bar. He wore a shabby poncho, and the tips of his long, greasy mustache were just visible, peeking out below a huge sombrero; the barkeep's head was lowered as he intently wiped and scrubbed at the chipped melamine bar. John made a face. "I imagine he only ever cleans that spot, but he does it *really* well."

Akane giggled. "I'd usually say 'Don't be mean,' but honestly, I'm worried we'll get stuck to this table and never be able to get out again."

"I swear I spotted McDonald's arches a few miles back down the highway," said Slack morosely. "Either that or we could order sandwiches from room service again."

"Room service would be safer," agreed Salome.

"No." John shook his head. "I told you we *had* to come in here. This isn't a whim, honest. That impulse—you know how it is? There's no resisting it. There's something in here for us—IIDA knows it, and so do I."

"You're sure the prompt came from IIDA?" asked Akane. "Because there's nobody here, unless they're hidden inside that ugly monster dinosaur at the door."

Anxious, John turned and scanned the dingy room. She was right. There wasn't another soul in the place.

He shrugged. "Then we have to wait. What do you want to eat?"

<31>

"In here?" Salome sniffed. "I'm not sure I want anything."

"*I* want a beer," announced Slack. "We might as well hang out at the bar, since he cleans that part." Marching between the tables, he pulled out a stool and hoisted himself onto it like a seasoned barfly as the others joined him. "A bottle of Corona, please, Miguel."

"Slack!" hissed Salome, horrified. "You're way too young!"

"Miguel won't care. Will you, Miguel?"

The sombrero didn't tilt upward, though the tips of that straggly mustache twitched. "I may be Miguel," growled a voice, "but that don't mean you're getting a beer."

"Hey, we're your only customers," said Slack cheerfully. "You might as well serve us."

There was silence beneath the sombrero. After a moment, the man rummaged beneath the bar and brought out a can of Coke and a smeared glass. He slammed them onto the bar. "Dollar ninety."

Slack gasped. "A dollar and ninety cents for warm Coke when I wanted a cold beer?"

"Correction." There was amusement in Miguel's rough voice. "For Ghosts, the warm soda is complimentary. At least, it is when they've completed a successful mission."

Salome gasped, and Akane gave a squeal of excitement. Slack gaped at Miguel, then slanted his eyes anxiously at John. John himself could only stare, his mind filled with a conflict of emotions.

"Dad?" he rasped.

Mikael Laine swept the sombrero from his head and gave a quick bow. Tossing the hat aside, he flipped one side of his

<32>

poncho onto his shoulder, leaned on the bar, and smiled at all of them.

"Sorry about the condition of the place," he said. "It's not like I'm here very often, and the staff have stopped caring. Or coming into work, for that matter." He gave a wry shrug.

"That's not the point of this place, though, is it?" Salome tilted her head and watched him admiringly. "It's just a cover. Or a dead drop, maybe?"

"Miguel. Mikael." Akane was laughing. "We should have guessed."

"I'm just glad I wasn't too obvious." Mikael peeled off the fake mustache and flicked it under the bar. "Hello, Son."

Despite his lighthearted demeanor, John could sense Mikael's wary anxiety. *And I'm not about to help him,* he thought bitterly. The surge of excitement at seeing his father conflicted with his raging resentment. Mikael's fingers twitched, and he moved a little toward John, but John remained impassive and unmoving, and his father drew back.

Mikael had changed a lot. But then John hadn't laid eyes on his dad for a year. He'd never expected to, ever again, since Mikael had let his whole family think he was *dead.* Dad looked thinner, thought John, and haggard, but he was very much alive. *And he let us grieve for him . . .*

"Nice to see you, Dad." His voice held almost steady. "Haven't seen you since Eagle Point in Utah. The Vertigo ski run, wasn't it? You were going fast, right from the top, when the avalanche struck."

"John, I—"

<33>

"And then you disappeared in the chaos, and we never saw you again."

Mikael gazed at him sadly. "I wanted to see you, John. You know why I couldn't."

Yes. He did. But it didn't make it hurt any less. John could only shrug.

The silence was horrific; of course it was Slack who broke it at last. "So did the Lucci Corp mission come from you, Mr. Laine?"

"Mikael, please." He looked relieved. "And, yes, that was your first test. Which you passed with flying colors, my Ghosts."

"Of course we did," remarked Slack smugly.

"Wait. It was just a test?" Salome folded her arms.

"Yes, but an important one. Don't get me wrong. I wanted to see whether you were up to a challenge because there will be much bigger ones down the line." Mikael rested his fists on the bar. "But, yeah, this was pretty routine compared to what I've got planned. You took down Lucci Corp—and Carl di Lucci, by the way. You know he's been called in by a Senate committee? A prosecution's inevitable. It's public knowledge now that Lucci Corp was falsifying information and handing out bribes to drill in one of the world's most treasured nature reserves. *You* exposed that." Leaning back, he folded his arms and added drolly, "Ideally, you wouldn't have stolen a hundred-thousand-dollar Tesla and attracted the attention of half the Alaska State Troopers, but I can't expect miracles." He rolled his eyes. "It's a learning process, I guess."

Picking up a battered remote, Mikael turned and switched on the small flat-screen behind the bar. The CNN anchor was mouthing something, silent but visibly excited, and footage of oil

<34>

wells and an expanse of tundra flashed up behind her. The ticker read *Di Lucci to testify before House committee. Lucci Corp share price in free fall.*

"You've made headline news." Leaving the TV on mute, Mikael clicked through the channels: ABC, Fox, NBC, CBS. All of them were running the same story. "The world may not know what part you played, you guys, but I do. I'm proud. And I'm grateful."

The tips of Slack's ears were red with excitement. He blew the blond fringe out of his eyes, grinning uncontrollably.

"If this is what we can do on a trial run," he yelled, banging his fist on the bar, "wait till the Ghost Network *really* gets started!"

The others had discarded all their suspicions about the food at Miguel's and were chomping greedily on fajitas, but John couldn't eat a single bite. He was trying not to stare resentfully at his father, but he couldn't help it; his appetite had disappeared.

"We're officially international Men of Mystery," declared Slack through a mouthful of chicken and chili.

"Men?" Salome arched a withering eyebrow. "Let me remind you who drove the car."

"*And* who retrieved the suitcase from the highway," added Akane, kicking Slack's shin.

"Don't get cocky, Slack," warned Mikael. "And that applies to all of you, however well you drive and pick locks." He smiled at Salome. "You're still in a pretty dangerous situation. It's not safe to go back to the Wolf's Den, not for the foreseeable future."

<35>

Slack paused, his mouth full. "But we will go back *eventually*. Right?"

"Doesn't bother me, since I've never even been there," said Akane. She shrugged, but she sounded a little sulky. "I don't see why you're all so attached to it, to be honest."

"Sorry, Akane. I know you didn't get to go there," said John, his eyes fixed on his father. "But we've got to go back. Eva is still there!"

"And we have to help her." Salome slapped her fajita back onto her plate, looking truculent. "That girl helped us escape Lykos."

"The Wolf's Den is *home*," said Slack firmly. "It just feels like home, and it did right from the start."

"Exactly," said Salome. "We belong there more than Lykos does!"

"*I* don't," growled Akane under her breath.

"Akane, you don't feel it yet," said Mikael, leaning on the bar, "but when you go there, you'll know what these three know. That you're in the right place. Salome, Slack, and John feel a strong connection to the Wolf's Den because their minds are assigned to its server. It's their link to IIDA—the supercomputer that's your second 'Mom.'" He smiled at her. "The Wolf's Den is their true home, their sanctuary, and one day you'll know it's yours too."

"Yeah, I'd like to feel that too." Akane folded her arms, avoiding the others' eyes.

"Not yet," Mikael told her firmly, drawing back to polish another glass. "Lykos now has full access to Lab 31, where the Center's supercomputer is. It won't be long before he has access to the operating system. That'll give him control of your AI—all of you."

<36>

All four Ghosts went quiet. After a long, subdued moment, Slack pushed back his barstool. "So Lykos is trying to hack the operating system so that he can control us. Do I have that right?"

Mikael nodded. "That's pretty much it."

"In that case," said Slack, "how long do we have?"

The other three turned to stare at Mikael, as the grim reality of their situation sank in.

"It's not possible," blurted Salome. "Lykos can't *control* me. I'm a person. I have my own thoughts. I have free will. Nobody can make me do something I don't want to do!"

Mikael averted his eyes. "It's not that simple, Salome. Yes, you'd fight it, but you know how slickly your programming goes into action. You could fight the impulses and the command prompts, but it'd be tough. And as your mind adapts and the prompts overwhelm your own system—as they eventually would—your programming would kick in spontaneously."

"In other words, we'd be essentially reprogrammed." Akane stared at Mikael.

Slowly, John shook his head in disgust. "What did you do to us, Dad? What did you think you were *doing*?"

Mikael met his eyes at last. He looked remorseful but defiant.

"I was saving your lives," he said quietly. "I didn't foresee the unintended consequences; that's true. But it was all I could do at the time. There seemed to be such possibilities."

"There certainly were," said Salome frostily.

Slack shot them all disapproving looks. "Well, I for one am glad to be alive," he declared. "And, what's more, it's exciting more than it's scary. But I'm going to ask again anyway." He turned back to Mikael. "How long do we have?"

<37>

Mikael took a deep breath. "I don't know," he said. "I estimate maybe two months."

"Two *months?*" gasped Salome in horror.

"There's something you're not telling us, Dad," growled John.

"Yes. There is." Mikael sighed. "Because I meant what I said: that two months is an estimate. And the truth is Lykos could break the encryption at any moment."

<38>

Five

"There's one thing I want you to know," said Mikael into the heavy, hopeless silence. John remembered that facial expression well; it was the bright-eyed, insistent look his father used to give them when they were hopelessly lost in the wilderness and couldn't find the map, and Mikael thought the next tiny mud track on the left would get them where they needed to be.

"What's that?" John asked, skeptically.

"Lykos has no way of finding your whereabouts—not till he breaks into that system and directly into you. So until that happens, Eva Vygotsky is safe."

Mikael nodded at Salome. "Roy won't harm her, first because she's another connection to you and, second, because she's in possession of the AI herself—or an untested version of it."

"You're sure he won't hurt her?" asked Salome, biting her lip.

"No way." Mikael shook his head. "She's too valuable to him. He values what's inside her, anyway. Please don't worry about Eva—because you're not going to have the mental energy to spare."

"What does that mean?" John narrowed his eyes.

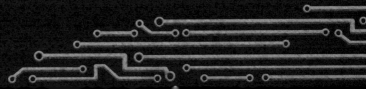

"It means we're going to take your training to the next level." Mikael straightened. "Roy will never stop coming after you, so there's only one thing you can do—and that's go after *him*. Now, you're not ready for that. You need to train to get to a level where you can safely take him on. You need to take back the Wolf's Den, and you need to do it before it's too late."

"I suppose we could take him on. Right *now*." Slack picked up his knife, flipped it in his palm, and, with a barely perceptible pause, turned and launched it with a smooth overarm motion at the plastic dinosaur. The knife flew straight and true, piercing the dinosaur between the eyes. It stuck there, quivering.

As they all stared at him, Slack turned back toward them and grinned.

"I couldn't throw a knife till right now. I accessed IIDA, and she showed me how. See? I expect we can do anything!"

Mikael gave him a rueful grin. "Yes. And you'd be flinging knives *on Roy Lykos's behalf* if you went in unprepared. My Ghosts, it's true: you can do pretty much anything, if you set your programming to it. Lykos can't do that; he doesn't have your abilities. But he does know how to harness IIDA. And he fully intends to do so. If he gets to you first, he'll be invincible. And he'll make *you* go into battle for him."

That silenced Slack. He stared at his plate.

"You *can* do anything, Slack," said Mikael gently. "But don't you want to do it for the good guys?"

"So long as we're sure who the good guys are," muttered John.

Salome gave him a sharp look. "I think we know that, John. After what happened to us at the Wolf's Den, I for one am certain enough." She turned back to Mikael. "So what's our next move?"

<40>

With an anxious glance at John, Mikael nodded. "You need the resources of IIDA to help further your training, but you need to access them somewhere else, somewhere Lykos can't. He and his acolytes have infiltrated almost every IIDA terminal in the world, but there's one Center he doesn't know about. It's called the Scarab's Temple. It's in the Sahara desert."

"Sounds . . . warmer than Alaska," said Slack hopefully.

"The Sahara," said John. He could feel a simmering anger rising inside his throat, threatening to choke him. "So I have to trek around the world again at your command. I've already chased my tail around North America for your benefit, and now you want to send me to a *desert*?" He stood up abruptly, clenching his fists.

"John, calm down," said Mikael.

"It took us all awhile to calm down when we found out you were *dead*," John gritted. "Me and Mom and Leona, that is."

Silence fell.

"You're looking good for a dead man," John went on. "Mom and Leona cried for days, you know." He wasn't going to admit that he had too.

"John," said Mikael softly, "I disappeared to protect you."

"But you're here now," spat John. "So why did you let us wait a whole year? Why do Mom and Leona *still* have to think you're dead?"

"If I told you that, someone could get *that* information from you." There was exasperation in Mikael's voice. "I'll explain one day, but—"

"Excuses, excuses." John gritted his teeth. "You've always got another one." It was all spilling out of him now, unstoppable grief and fury. "Mikael Laine, you're a *liar*."

<41>

Mikael stared at John, his eyes wide and dark with hurt. Salome focused her eyes on the countertop; Akane fixed hers on the muted TV. Slack fiddled with the remains of his fajita, shredding it with fierce concentration.

John swallowed hard. He knew he should regret his outburst, but he really didn't.

"If there was so much danger," he murmured, "why didn't you take the initiative and go after Lykos yourself? Why did you have to wait for me and my friends to find out we're freaks? Freaks *you* created. Why didn't *you* have the guts to destroy Lykos?"

Mikael took a slight step forward. He looked as if he wanted to reach out, but the countertop was between them, and John was glad. "He was *Roy Lykos*. Do you know how many friends he has in high places?"

"Governments change," seethed John.

"I don't just mean politicians—I mean lobbyists, the media, blue ticks on Twitter. If I'd stepped up and accused him, not one of them would have believed me. Would *you* have believed me, before all this happened?"

John stared at him in silence.

"Lykos is practically a god in the tech world," Mikael went on, "and those are people who have at least an inkling of what he can do. To the wider population he's a saint with his charity work, educational trusts, and a bestselling memoir with an adaptation on Netflix. He sends free tech into schools. He was invited to the last royal wedding, for Pete's sake." Mikael's growl took on an edge of bitterness. "Journalists love him, and so does everyone else. He's a global superstar, and he's untouchable."

<42>

"No one is untouchable," said John quietly. "Remember Achilles? Big hero, crucial to the whole cause, unbeatable. Till Paris shot an arrow into his heel."

"Yes, that's what I'm hoping for." Mikael shrugged. "That Lykos has a vulnerability. I just have to find out where it is."

"No," said John, drawing himself up and looking straight into his father's eyes. "I do. *We* do. Your Ghost Network."

"Remember why Achilles had that weak spot, John?"

"'Course I do," said John. "His mom dipped him in the Styx to make him invulnerable, but she forgot to dip his heel."

Mikael nodded. "And there has to be something in Roy Lykos's past too."

"Yes," said John. "There does. Something that'll let us get to him. I swear it."

A hush fell again, and for the first time, father and son watched each other without hostility. John felt a lump in his throat. *I'm still mad at him. But he's my dad.* It wasn't his father who was his true enemy, thought John: it was Roy Lykos.

Mikael looked away. "I believe you, John. I completely believe you'll beat him. But it's going to put you in danger, and I'm sorry for that—more sorry than you can imagine." He drew a breath. "With every step you take now, you have to consider first how it could potentially help Lykos track you down. To start with, you can't contact anyone outside this circle. Do you understand? Anyone. It would be a huge risk to you, but it would also put *them* in danger. Your friends, their families."

Salome nodded seriously. "We understand. No outside contact."

<43>

"So how am I going to explain to my mom that I'm going to the Sahara?" asked Slack dryly. "Am I supposed to tell her I'm going to research camels?"

"I've heard worse excuses," laughed Mikael, "but a field trip to Arizona would be more believable, so that's the story I want you to use. You're going to study mesa formation, with a view to developing computer models for predicting erosion. That should be detailed enough to satisfy even the most curious of your families."

Slack tilted his head thoughtfully. "Fair enough. And I'm sure John can convince his mom," he added mischievously. "I mean, Tina thought an animated headshot was actually Roy Lykos himself."

A flicker of pain crossed Mikael's face at the mention of his wife's name, but it was gone quickly. "Another thing: when you get to the Scarab's Temple, don't even think about using the computers there to contact students elsewhere." He gestured at Salome, meeting her tormented gaze. "Don't try to contact Eva. You can't access the IIDA mainframe without every other computer in the network knowing it."

Salome nodded reluctantly.

Slack rolled his eyes. "Sure, Mikael. I'm glad you explained that about the network, because we're complete computer noobs."

Mikael laughed. "Fair enough. But it's like the safety demo when you get on a plane: even the frequent flyers should watch it."

Slack slipped down from his barstool. "I guess if I'm really not getting a beer, we should get going. No time to waste and all that."

<44>

"You're not getting a beer," confirmed Mikael, "and, yes, there's no time like the present."

Salome retreated to one of the booths, one with a featureless backdrop, to Skype her parents. Slack pulled his phone from his pocket. Akane unpacked her laptop and found a booth of her own.

"I should call Mom," John told Mikael, a little awkward now that they were alone.

"Yes. I don't want her to worry any more than she already does." Mikael gazed at him. "But there's something else I wanted to give you. It might be useful." He rummaged behind the counter, then walked around the bar to John's side.

What sophisticated tech was Mikael going to give him? John wondered. Despite his lingering resentment, he felt a spark of excitement. *A new burner phone, one with capabilities I've never heard of? A tracker device? A jet pack would be nice . . .*

"Here." Mikael extended his hand.

John stared at the thing in his father's palm. It was a small, lumpy block of black plastic with a single green screen and a few buttons.

"What in the name of Odin is *that* thing?" he asked, wrinkling his nose.

Mikael chuckled. "It's what we considered high tech in the '90s. It's a pager, John. Primitive, but it works, and it doesn't use IIDA networks. If there's an emergency, and if you think there's any chance Lykos has broken IIDA's encryption, this is how you can reach me. OK?"

John took the pager. "It even has a belt hook," he said, rolling his eyes. "What'll they think of next?"

<45>

They both laughed, and for a moment John forgot how bitter he felt. It was almost like old times, he thought: *when Dad would explain stuff to me and I thought he was the most brilliant, wisest, smartest man on the planet.*

He sighed and looked up. "Thanks, Dad."

Mikael reached out to pull him into a hug.

"Thank you, John. For trusting me, *for now*." Mikael's eyes looked tormented. "Now call your mom. Tell her you'll be safe. And to keep you that way, I'll get you on that plane to Morocco."

<46>

Six

There was nothing Eva Vygotsky wanted more than to climb the stairs to the outside world, stand on the windswept plateau of Little Diomede Island, and let the Arctic breeze chill her body and clear her head. She wanted to see the sky and the choppy sea and the lumpy outline of Big Diomede, barely a stone's throw away but just across the dateline in Russian waters. She wanted to leave the Wolf's Den complex beneath her feet, just for half an hour. Was that really too much to ask?

Apparently, yes. She had been confined within the Wolf's Den's interior since the night her friends John, Slack, and Salome had escaped. Her every move, her every look was monitored by the cameras that rotated silently in the corner of every room. She knew it and could say nothing. There was no family for her to return to, no place for her to go. She did not trust a single member of the staff. The Wolf's Den was her home—the only one she had ever known—but now she feared she might never be able to leave.

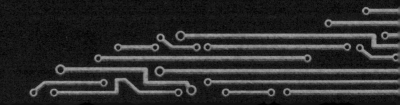

She didn't know whether she could stand it. Especially when she had to sit here, stuck in a whole-school assembly in the main lecture theater, being talked at by Irma Reiffelt.

"At this Center, ladies and gentlemen, you will learn to protect individuals and computing systems against those who would do them harm." Pause for dramatic effect. "Unless, of course, *we want* you to do them harm."

There was a nervous ripple of laughter from the new students, and Eva tried not to roll her eyes. It was Ms. Reiffelt's standard beginning-of-term lecture, and the older students must have been even more bored than Eva was.

Eva stole a glance at some of the noobs. John Laine did not like her to use that term—he thought it was demeaning—but there was really no other word that fit. They looked so eager, so innocent; not one of them had any idea of the chaos that had happened last term. Roy Lykos and his teacher cronies had covered it all up very effectively: nothing had leaked online, and not a single press organization or anarchic blogger knew that helicopters had flown in to abduct three of the students or that Roy Lykos had conspired to steal the intellectual property that was woven into those students' DNA. It was not public knowledge that guns had been drawn in an elite hacking school. And the very existence of John Laine and his friends Slack and Salome had apparently been wiped from the school's history.

Eva tried, not very successfully, to suppress a sigh. She sat several rows back from the main student body, alone and isolated. That was her choice. She couldn't remember when she'd last spoken voluntarily to another student—certainly never outside class. She certainly had no desire to talk to Adam Kruz or

<48>

Leo Pallikaris, who sat sprawled out in their chairs at the front, looking superior and smug. She would never forgive those two rich boys for siding with Lykos, for betraying her friends—and, most of all, for booby-trapping her laptop with their stupid virus and threatening to destroy all her data. And the boys were as stupid as their malware: poisoning Eva's computer data didn't just threaten her work; it endangered her actual mind.

Adam and Leo couldn't have known; they weren't in on Mikael Laine's AI project. But being outwitted by John and the others had not dented their arrogance one bit. And Eva would not ever feel like forgiving them.

Eva blinked, realizing that Irma Reiffelt had left the podium to make way for Roy Lykos. The tech superstar (and all-around thug and psycho, thought Eva bitterly) was taking the steps two at a time: slim and athletic but austere and dressed in his usual black. He wore a thin-lipped smile as he reached the podium and gazed out at his new student intake. They stared back with a mixture of awe and sheer adoration.

If only they knew, thought Eva.

"Thank you, Ms. Reiffelt," Lykos said with a nod toward the principal. "I know everyone here is more than ready to begin their term's work. I've spoken to many of you already, and you've turned up with exactly the right mind-set: inquiring, curious, and determined to learn. That's what we at the Wolf's Den want most in our students, and you are all more than welcome!"

A burst of wondering applause broke out at his banal little speech, and Eva glared at the shiny-eyed students.

Lykos waited for the applause to die down and nodded solemnly. "There's so much we offer here, and I want you all to

<49>

make the most of every opportunity—for study, for relaxation, for individual enterprise. I expect to see great things from all of you. But as you can imagine from an elite institution, we demand dedication too. It's not all fun and fully interactive virtual-reality climbing walls!" He gave them a grin and a wink that sent a few of them into spasms of giggles—deep down, he was still a nerd, Eva thought—then he grew serious again. "We demand dedication, and hard work, and loyalty to the Wolf's Den. Sadly, I can't tell you that this has always been the case."

Oh, thought Eva, stiffening. *Here it comes.*

Lykos sighed. "Last term, we lost some highly promising students. Despite their intelligence and creativity, they were unable to operate under the Wolf's Den's strict code of conduct. It broke my heart, let me tell you, but we had to say goodbye to those students."

There were a few gasps of disbelief and outrage from the audience.

"Imagine," whispered a girl to her neighbor, two rows in front of Eva. "Imagine having this kind of privilege and abusing it!" She sounded horrified.

Eva bit her lip hard and said nothing.

"I'm sorry to have to make this part of my welcome address," Lykos went on, lowering his eyes to a card that he pulled from his pocket. "But I mean it when I say these students were talented. They were among the most promising students we've ever had— not that we could allow that to sway our decision, unfortunately. And it's possible they might still try to make mischief. You're all tech-savvy enough to imagine the ways they might do that. So should any of you . . . *any of you*"—his gaze drifted dangerously

<50>

close to Eva—"receive any form of contact from the following, you are obliged to report it to me. And I mean to *me* personally. The names are as follows: John Laine, Jake Hook, Salome Abraham. And there's another name, one who failed to qualify for entrance and who is alarmingly bitter about that: Akane Maezono."

Eva felt a surge of anger, and she had to fight not to scream out loud. *You liar! Akane never failed any entrance exam—you just hadn't gotten to her yet!* And just as well Lykos hadn't gotten his claws into Akane, she reflected: last term it was Akane who had met the other three on the outside and helped them to escape across the frozen wasteland of Alaska.

Roy Lykos was folding up the card, meticulously and rather sternly. He ran a fingernail firmly along the crease he'd made. "Any contact must, I repeat, *must* be reported to me. *Immediately.* Or there will be consequences, whether you are a co-conspirator or the innocent recipient of an unsolicited message. Do you all understand?"

Eva studied him as the assembled students murmured their nervous agreement. His mask of a friendly and stern-but-approachable genius had slipped just for a moment; Lykos looked for a fleeting moment like the amoral, emotionless psychopath she knew him to be. Behind his wire-framed glasses, his steely eyes flashed frozen daggers.

Then, in a flash, the warm and kindly teacher returned. "That's good. If I know anything about this student body, it's that you're all smart and you understand the outcomes of batch command sequences." He grinned, and there was a low hubbub of laughter as the tension ebbed. "I'm glad to have you all here, and I have

<51>

some exciting new projects to tell you about. You all know how much more concerned governments have become in recent years, how much more aware they are of digital threats and the dangers of cyber warfare. Well, as of last week, the Wolf's Den is teaming up with the US government, and together we're declaring war on cyberterrorism!"

This time the assembly lost all their shyness; they cheered and clapped their excitement and approval.

"I'll be personally selecting an elite class of hackers; your mission will be to quash genuine, real-world threats. These won't be war games or virtual exercises in our simulated world, Global One. This, for the best students, will be *real.*"

The whole assembly erupted. Around Eva she could hear the eager chatter of students determined to make it into Roy Lykos's elite class; she felt a pang of sorrow as she remembered John and Slack's excitement last term, their determination to be chosen for Lykos's special lessons.

If they'd arrived this term, they'd have been joining in, she thought. *Maybe I would have fought for the chance myself, when I first came here.*

The irony was it was clear what Lykos meant by *genuine, real-world threats.* He meant John and Slack themselves. And Salome and Akane. *The Ghost Network.* They'd once been star students; now they might as well have a giant digital target fixed on their backs.

Eva had known an outburst like that speech was coming. Of course Lykos couldn't carry on indefinitely as if nothing had happened. He must still feel under threat. And he was human,

<52>

despite all his technological brilliance, but he had some of the worst traits of a human.

Like a thirst for revenge . . .

She should feel dread and fear, but Eva only felt numb. *I have to do something. I have to. I just don't know what.*

She barely heard the rest of the assembly speeches. When it was over, she rose with the rest of the student body, gathered her books and laptop, and made her way in a daze back to her room.

She'd agreed with the Ghost Network that she'd carry on as if nothing had happened. She'd continue with her schooling, pretend everything was normal, and lie low. But how could she keep that promise now? Lykos was making his move, and her friends were in mortal danger. *I have to do something!*

She lifted her wrist implant, and the door of her room slid smoothly open. Eva stepped inside, still distracted and wracked with concern, and then heard the door slide shut behind her.

There was something different about the sound as it clicked into place. Frowning, Eva turned and faced the door. It was featureless, pale wood; she'd always found it stylish, but now she couldn't help seeing something sinister in its blankness.

Eva lifted her wrist. Nothing. This was new.

She pressed her wrist to the door. She backed up a good distance and tried again.

These implants did not malfunction. They just didn't. A tide of panic washed through her body, and her blood ran cold. With a strangled yell, Eva slammed her wrist against the door.

It stayed put. And so, apparently, must she.

Eva did not know which was stronger: her rage or her terror. Her roaming gaze must have seen too much; she must have

<53>

stared too long and coldly at a tutor. She'd helped the Ghost Network, and she'd refused to disown them afterward. Her hostility, her noncompliance, had been noted, and they had decided it was time for a crackdown.

She was Roy Lykos's prisoner.

<54>

Seven

The last plane flight John had taken had been with his family, from Vancouver to Alaska, and he barely remembered it. He'd been in a fog of grief after the "death" of his father. *It was Dad who inflicted that on me.*

No, he must try to forget that; he had to look forward. On that flight he couldn't remember what movie he'd watched. Had there even been any? This flight was a lot rowdier—the group of young women sitting behind him were overly excited about their vacation—and he was glad for his earphones filled with the crash and racket of the movie he'd chosen. In the seat beside him, Slack was riveted by his screen.

Slack had the right idea; there was no point in worrying about what awaited them in Morocco. Frowning, John tried to concentrate on the antics of Thor and Rocket Raccoon. He'd waited ages to see this movie, and he might as well enjoy it.

Just as he decided that, the screen blanked out. Irritated, John tapped it. Nothing. He glanced at Slack, who had turned to him in surprised annoyance. His screen was dead too, John noticed. On the other side of the aisle, Salome and Akane were pulling off their earphones and muttering to one another; Akane actually grabbed the headrest in front of her and shook it. Leaning forward, John peered between the seats at the passenger screens in front. They were working perfectly. John leaned back, reaching up for the flight attendant button.

Just as he was about to press it, his screen burst back to life. So did Slack's. Salome and Akane leaned forward in their seats, replacing their earphones.

A slightly pixelated face appeared, instantly recognizable. John felt a small jolt in his chest yet again.

"Hello, Ghosts," smiled Mikael. "I'm sorry to interrupt your in-flight entertainment, but it's important to brief you."

Beside John, Slack rolled his eyes. "That was just at an exciting part," he muttered. "I hope your dad's gonna be quick."

"Morocco is where you're going to achieve your full potential." Mikael's voice was speaking over a touristy video of desert vistas, temples, and antiquities. "The Scarab's Temple has been given a mission, and that's to make you fully superhuman." Mikael's face reappeared. He looked solemn, his blue eyes unusually dark. "Until now, you've effectively been at the whim of fortune; you've had to wait and hope for communications from IIDA. Now you have to learn to be proactive. You have to learn to control your bodies and minds to adapt to your external environment. To access IIDA's power at your own will. You'll learn to unite, like a true network, to work as a single unstoppable force."

Mikael paused, and a headshot of Roy Lykos flickered briefly onto the screen. With a sudden feeling of dread, John exchanged a look with Slack.

<56>

Then Mikael was back. "I don't want to ruin your flight altogether," he grinned, "but that was just a quick reminder of what you're up against. Roy Lykos has powerful connections, right up to the ear of the president—and not just our own US president either. He also has the vast processing power of the Wolf's Den at his fingertips."

Mikael paused. His heart sinking, John raked a hand through his hair, nearly dislodging an earphone.

"But never forget this," Mikael went on, his gaze piercing despite the poor image quality. "Roy Lykos is one man, and he can only travel at the speed of his computer's processing power. You four have the advantage over him. At full force, you'll be making decisions and solving problems before Roy has even thought about his attack. Keep that in mind."

Slack grinned at John. Yes, thought John. *That does sound more hopeful.*

"All right." Mikael pushed his hands through his hair, unintendedly mimicking John. "One straightforward practicality. At the airport you'll be met by a man called Youssef; he'll be holding a sign that says 'Sahara Sunrise Holidays.' Go with him, and do whatever he says. I trust you. You're going to be an unstoppable force. Good luck, guys."

The screen cut out again. Before John could say anything to Slack, their movies were up and running once again. Slack relaxed in his seat, grinning, fully focused on the Avengers again.

He's so chill, thought John. He wished he could be half as cool as his friend. Maybe now would be a good time to start. Clenching and unclenching his fists, taking a deep breath, John tried to concentrate on the screen.

<57>

And it went blank again.

John blinked and glanced at Slack's. But his friend's movie was still running, and Iron Man and Spider-Man were battling it out with Thanos. Confused, John turned back to his own screen. Maybe this time it really was his fault?

Mikael's image smiled at him, a little sadly. "Just you and me this time, John. No need to alert the others."

"Dad," mouthed John, though he knew his father couldn't hear him.

"I don't like how we left things back at the restaurant, Son." Mikael took a deep breath. "I need to talk to you, and this is as good a place as any, because you won't be able to yell at me." He hesitated. "I want you to know I'm sorry, John. I'm sorry for how I handled things. And I need to explain it all to you, about why I went missing.

"I need to tell you what happened."

I didn't have a choice, John. Roy would have killed us all. What started as small differences on how to handle IIDA and the Centers grew into a lethal battle.

I told him about my plans for the Ghost Network, John. It was my biggest mistake, and it haunts me to this day. We were on a break, drinking coffee, leaning against our desks, half the lab lights off—I remember every detail of that night because it's stayed with me. I thought Roy was a good man. We were like brothers. I trusted him with my work, my life, my secrets.

<58>

So maybe I'm not a great judge of character. Maybe that's an understatement.

Then, he told me what he wanted out of Phase 2.

I won't go into the details right now, but it froze my blood. It's enough to say that he wanted to use you kids for his own purposes—create a private army to do his bidding. I told Roy right away that our joint project was off, that I'd never trust him with the full details of the Ghost Network. He was deeply hurt and upset—or he pretended to be. I don't think Roy Lykos truly feels emotions like that.

I don't think you remember this next part, John, because you've never spoken of it. When you were young, you had that miraculous ability children have to block out bad memories. A fire broke out at our house. Your mother and I, we were awoken by smoke at 3:00 a.m., and we only just got you and your sister out.

And the irony is it was Roy who helped us escape. Maybe that fire was only meant as a warning? As we were stumbling from the back porch of that old house and the flames were taking hold behind us, who should happen to be passing by? Roy said he'd driven over to discuss business, but I never believed him, not for a moment. He was there, John, the night our house caught fire, and that was when I knew we were all in mortal danger.

I had to do something. I didn't mean it to be at the slopes in Utah, John; I really didn't. When I said goodbye to you on Eagle Point, I fully expected to see you again. I thought we'd meet at the bottom of the Vertigo run.

There was a small avalanche. It wasn't a bad one, but it drove me off course. You, I think, barely noticed it; I think even then

<59>

you used the instincts I planted with your tech DNA to avoid it. You did it completely unconsciously. But I was caught up and driven off course. I was wearing my avalanche jacket, and I knew I'd be fine. But I got lost.

I made my own way out of the mountains that night, nearly dying of hypothermia. I could see the helicopters, and I knew you and Mom and Leona must be crazy with worry. But I didn't have any way of knowing whether the choppers were Mountain Rescue or whether they had something to do with Roy. I didn't want to end up falling out of one, so I hid from them as they passed. I'm sorry.

I wasn't being paranoid, John. I checked later that week; I hacked into systems, just the way you used to do. One of those helicopters was Mountain Rescue. But there were three. The other two—they weren't trying to save my life. They were aiming to end it.

I knew I had to go into hiding. It was going to be temporary. I thought I'd fix everything; I thought I'd be home soon enough for you all to rage at me and then forgive me. But it didn't work out that way. Roy thought I was dead, but he couldn't prove it, and he was tracking down all traces of me.

Roy was obsessed. I couldn't let him find out I was alive. And the absolute last thing I could let him do was get to me by hurting all of you. If you and Mom and Leona had known I wasn't dead, then Roy would have found out, and his methods are not civilized. I couldn't let it happen. Even if he'd left you alive, John—because he wanted what's inside you—he'd have killed your mom and sister.

<60>

But I watched you, John. I was always watching the three of you, from a distance. I promise I was protecting you.

I wish our lives had been different, Son. I wish I'd had a choice. I wish you'd never fallen from those rocks when you were barely more than a baby. I wish I hadn't had to do what I did to save your life. And I wish more than anything that I'd never been dumb enough to trust Roy Lykos.

But we choose our path, and sometimes there's no turning back.

Sometimes we have to keep following it to its end, even when we don't know where the end is or what's going to happen to us there.

I'm sorry, John.

And I love you.

click

<<>>

The image of his father, already pixelated, blurred in John's vision completely. *The fire. How could I have forgotten?* He could smell thick black smoke, as clearly and strongly as if the airplane cabin was full of it. Terrifying memories overwhelmed him, as if someone had keyed in a password and the files were downloading in an unstoppable torrent. Maybe someone had. *But I thought . . . I thought it was a dream! Oh, Dad.*

John rubbed his eyes hard. His heart was throbbing too hard to let him breathe properly. He couldn't help sniffing, gulping to repress a sob, and Slack nudged him.

<61>

John turned, blinking.

"How traumatic was *that*?" Slack's eyes brimmed. "I can't believe it ended that way. Groot! *Spider-Man!*"

John stared at him for a moment, then burst into unsteady laughter. "No spoilers!"

"Huh?" Slack frowned.

"Never mind. Yeah, it was pretty emotional." John took a deep, steadying breath. "Are we landing *already*?"

Slack peered past him out of the window. "Looks like it!"

Below the aircraft's wing lay roads, broad fields, and the geometric pattern of Casablanca's streets. A dusty golden light blanketed the drab suburbs and the airport terminal, making them almost dreamlike. Before John could get a good look— Slack was stretched across him, blocking the view—he felt the wheels bump down, and the morning sun glistened on the edges of the aircraft's flaps. The plane had barely skidded to a halt before Slack was out of his seat, yanking excitedly at his luggage stored in the overhead bin.

"This is going to be great!" he gushed. "Look at the weather out there. This beats Little Diomede!"

Locking eyes across the aisle with Salome, John felt a lot more apprehensive than his friend did. What exactly would this training involve if it was meant to unlock all their potential? How remote did a Center have to be to make it impossible for Roy Lykos to get his hands on them? Was there even such a location on planet Earth?

And, if so, just how far away *was* the Scarab's Temple?

<62>

"Seven hours' drive," said their contact cheerfully, lowering his Sahara Sunrise Holidays placard as he answered John's first nervous question. "I suggest you all use the airport bathroom facilities before we depart."

"Seven *hours?*" Akane's jaw dropped along with her backpack.

Youssef shrugged, grinning. "You could've caught an internal flight to Zagora, but that would have had you stuck in the airport lounge for a *lot* longer. Too much opportunity for you all to get lost. And this way, you get to see more of the country. Salaam, and welcome to Morocco!"

"Thanks," said John. "We're pretty excited."

"We'll have plenty of time to get to know one another on the journey." Youssef grinned again and grabbed Salome's bag in one hand, Akane's in the other.

"Thank you," said Salome breathlessly.

Youssef was maybe in his late twenties, John suspected. However, his face creased with deep dimples when he smiled, making his eyes almost disappear beneath his straight black brows. Salome looked a little smitten already.

As they walked through the terminal doors, they met a wall of heat, and they all paused for a moment, blinking in the golden sunlight. They shaded their eyes as they followed Youssef out to the parking lot.

"Don't suppose you've got an air-conditioned Tesla?" joked Slack.

"Better." Youssef swept out his arm, pointing to a slightly battered Land Rover Defender. "Better for desert driving, anyway."

He laughed uproariously at Akane's face. "Hey, it's more comfortable than it looks, *habibi*!"

"OK," said Akane guardedly. She clambered into the back, letting Salome take the passenger seat in front. John and Slack stowed their backpacks, then climbed in after Akane.

Youssef was right, John realized quickly: the Defender wasn't the rattletrap he'd expected. Youssef drove smoothly and confidently through the bustling streets of the city, occasionally gesturing from the open window.

"That big minaret, you see it? The Hassan II Mosque. The tallest minaret in the world! You can see it from pretty much everywhere in the city. Look, I'm going to take a detour through the center—the art deco architecture is really worth seeing."

John leaned out of the window, inhaling the smells as Youssef negotiated the crowds that filled the spice souk. He could make out the sharp tang of mint as well as rosemary, as pungent as his mother's kitchen when she was roasting lamb, and he felt a pang of fleeting homesickness. There were warmer, deeper scents of cumin, coriander, and a hundred other spices he couldn't name—and, beneath it all, smells that were a lot less pleasant. The shouts and jeers of the market traders and their customers were an assault on his ears, but he found he didn't mind.

"It's a long way from Alaska," he shouted with a grin, pulling his head back into the car.

"It's amazing," said Salome, her eyes gleaming with excitement. "Whoa, cinnamon! Smells all Christmassy."

"Yeah, amazing," groaned Slack, wrinkling his nose as they passed a drain. "Phew! Hey, Youssef," he added mischievously, "how about Rick's Café, can we see that?"

<64>

Youssef half turned, amused, as he blared his horn at obstructive pedestrians. "Sure, we can! Yes, it *does* exist outside the movie. I'll drive you past it. It's between the Medina and the Port . . ."

"It's not *all* unfamiliar." Salome pointed. There was a tinge of disappointment in her sigh as they drove past the familiar golden arches.

"Everybody comes to Casablanca, *habibi*," chuckled Youssef. "Including Ronald McDonald."

He seemed to have an endless supply of tour-guide banter. John was half disappointed, half relieved when the Defender finally lurched onto a main artery road and the city with its sights, noises, and scents shrank in the rearview. Youssef swiftly left the highways behind to follow a straight, dusty road through green fields.

There had been so many people swarming through the city streets, and John couldn't help feeling a lingering tinge of anxiety on the back of his neck. *I don't think cities are the best place for us right now, Youssef . . .* It would be way too easy for Lykos or his minions to track them down in a big town.

That reminded him of his father's warnings—and of his final gift. Tugging the old-fashioned pager from his pocket, John turned it curiously between his fingers. What an antique. At least it didn't look difficult to operate.

"What's that?" Slack peered down at it.

"Something, uh . . . something I found." John shot his friend a look of warning. Youssef hadn't mentioned Mikael yet, and John wasn't even sure his father's continued existence was common knowledge among Center staff.

<65>

Glancing up, he noticed Youssef's dark eyes fixed on him in the rearview mirror. "What is that you've got?"

"Uh, nothing," said John. He liked Youssef, but if the Wolf's Den had taught him anything, it was to give his trust sparingly.

"Sorry, I'm a bit embarrassed," he said, thinking quickly. "It's an in-flight remote. I thought it might be useful, so I stole it from the plane."

The driver threw back his head and roared with laughter. "I'm sure the airline can afford to lose it."

Youssef turned his attention back to the road and to Salome, answering her questions and making her giggle. Slack gave John a quizzical look, but John shook his head.

He felt bad about telling even the smallest lie to the friendly and vocal Youssef, but he couldn't help himself. Maybe that was one of the biggest downsides of being a Ghost. Maybe he was becoming suspicious and paranoid. It made him sad, but he couldn't help it. It was better than the alternative, John reminded himself: that maybe not everyone was on their side.

Trust no one.

<66>

Eight

It turned out Eva wasn't restricted to her room, she
discovered, but the door did unlock itself only at specific times.
No more random lunches or snack breaks for her, and no more
sudden hankerings for late-night sushi—she ate when she got
the chance, at boringly regular meal times. And, of course, she
was allowed to attend classes, but even there, she was constantly
aware of being watched.

It wasn't always the teachers doing the watching; there were
cameras everywhere, and she knew they were focused on her.
Eva still had a mind of her own—it was one thing Roy Lykos
couldn't control, at least for now—and she could make her own
observations and deductions.

Not all of the teachers were in on Lykos's conspiracy; she was
sure of it. Howard McAuliffe and Imogen Black, Eva believed,
were not even aware that Roy was restricting her freedom or
tracking her every move. She wasn't so certain about Irma Reiffelt
and Yasuo Yamamoto, though. Irma's face was always so
impassive that there was no way to tell what was going on in
her head. And Eva didn't want to believe that Yasuo, with his

warm smile and easygoing nature, was in on Lykos's conspiracy. However, she was no longer so confident as she'd once been. Too many times in class she'd seen his gaze slide toward her, his brow furrowed slightly in what looked like apprehension or maybe disapproval.

Whoever the bad guys are, they watch me, Eva thought as she stared at the homework hacking challenge on her laptop. *But they can't see inside my head.*

At least, she hoped not. She had only a vague idea of what had happened to John, Slack, and Salome when they were young, but she knew genetically altered tissue was present in her own brain. Maybe one day the bad guys *would* be able to hack into her head. But for now, Lykos had been thwarted. The Ghost Network had seen to that.

She was running against the clock, but she was still running, still winning. And she had enough natural-born genius and AI-given instinct to give her an edge.

You think you can recruit kids as smart as me and not have us bite you in the butt? thought Eva with a satisfied little smirk. Then she glowered at the locked door of her room. *You don't know how wrong you are, Roy Lykos.*

Flexing her fingers, then stretching her arms, she closed her homework assignment and once again began tapping on her keyboard.

Plan B?

<68>

Eva kicked back her chair and jumped to her feet, clenching her fists in frustration. Of course these creeps were going to have a plan B. Maybe in the back of her head she'd realized that all along, but seeing it there in Yasuo's files was like a punch to the gut.

Yasuo Yamamoto and Roy Lykos were both—what was it Slack called them? *Squillionaires.* Eva had always thought that word was hilarious. It didn't seem so funny now. They didn't need money funneling through official Wolf's Den channels, not when Yasuo could finance their whole secretive research project.

Yes. It looked like Yasuo was one of the bad guys. *Not Yasuo— Yamamoto*, Eva angrily rechristened him in her head.

Sitting down again and taking deep breaths, she stared fixedly at the downloaded files. The decrypted list scrolled upward under her quick fingers.

Lee Minseo

Wu Bao

Leanne Winchester

Devon Ifill

Ion Anghelescu

Baxter McCain

Tanya Kuznetsov

Eva was more than familiar with the names. They were the fastest hackers in the school, the best tacticians, the systems analysts with the sharpest instincts. These students were the elite squad of an elite school.

But she was most familiar with the final name on the list, the one in square brackets:

[Eva Vygotsky]

<69>

Those brackets made her spine shudder. She was different, Eva knew that already, but it was clear they had her marked down as such.

She rubbed her temples. What was she? A rogue element? She wasn't distinguished from the others because of some lack of ability; she had enough confidence to know *that*.

Was she less important than the others? Or *more* important?

A bug, a glitch? Eva felt a sudden pang of certainty. That had to be it. *Ghost in the machine.* But why? What was it about her that merited those sinister brackets?

She'd been one of Mikael's earliest experiments, so Eva assumed she'd had some life-threatening crisis early in her young life. The trouble was she didn't know what it had been. Her memories began on that trans-Siberian train where they'd found her. Passed from department to department, from one international legal force to another, she'd ended up at the Wolf's Den, and for a while she'd found peace and the isolation she loved.

But there was something wrong with her, that Eva was certain of. The way Adam and Leo's malware had affected her via her laptop; the skull-crushing headaches that seemed too skillfully timed to be natural. Her AI treatment had been the 1.0 version. Something had gone wrong. And those square brackets told her that Lykos didn't know either.

But he wants me here, and not because he likes me. He needs something from me.

Frowning, Eva clicked through to the financial plans: where was Yamamoto getting the cash flow for whatever he planned? Squillionaire he might be, but not all his assets could be liquid.

<70>

No, there it was, a footnote in the shape of a simple Excel document: the plan to mine Bitcoin exchanges, undetected. Eva allowed herself a tiny, satisfied smile.

"Recruit the best, Lykos," she whispered to the computer, "and you and Yamamoto better watch your electronic backs."

Once again, she minimized a window and clicked on the more detailed plans. None of it seemed to make sense, but she had a more or less photographic memory. If she stored this in her brain, she could ask the Ghost Network, if she ever saw them again . . . *No.* She shouldn't think like that. When she saw her friends again, they would work out together what Lykos and Yamamoto were up to.

A cold shudder rippled through her. How long could her friends stay safe, with those two hunting them? Eva dreaded to think what might happen if Lykos got control of the Ghost Network. She was stuck here on a remote island, the captive of Lykos, while John, Slack, and Salome tried to dodge his searching tentacles. *He can't get ahold of them. He just can't.* But what could she do to help prevent that from here?

Eva hated Lykos all the more for making her feel so unusually helpless. *He can't have me either. I don't care what he does; I won't ever work for him. And I won't let him get his claws into my friends.*

The screen blurred in front of Eva's eyes. She was so, so tired. Drowsily, she blinked. *I could fall asleep right here.*

No. She *was* asleep. At least, the conscious part of her brain was. Eva felt a sort of helpless, paralyzed numbness, even as something else, something subconscious, sparked to life in her head. To all outward appearance, she must have looked almost comatose, but it was as if programs were running, constant and

<71>

insistent in the background. Command prompts flashed by unseen; reams of data flickered across her synapses.

Eva felt a surge of helpless horror. *IIDA!* She was sure it was the Mother Computer. Was this what John felt when IIDA accessed his brain?

It was *horrible.* There was no resisting it: the program ripped through the information on the screen in front of her, analyzing, compressing, selecting, and interpreting. Data poured into her brain in a torrent.

Upload complete

She was terrified.

Commence decryption

And she couldn't move a muscle.

Analysis 70% done

She wanted to move her fingers, wanted to shut down the laptop, but even that small movement was beyond her.

Analysis 98% done

Please stop, please stop

Analysis complete

This time, Eva sprang up so abruptly that her chair tumbled over. Gripping the edge of the desk, she panted for breath. Her mind had the information she needed now—even if she didn't want it.

"You criminal jerks," she whimpered, barely audibly.

If Lykos and Yamamoto couldn't have the Ghost Network, they'd make their own. The kids on the regular list were the subjects.

And the one in square brackets . . . Eva herself . . . this was why they were holding on to her. Thanks to IIDA, she knew it swiftly

<72>

and for certain. She was plan B: they needed what was inside her. She was going to be used for data harvesting. For DNA harvesting. If all else failed, if Lykos and Yamamoto couldn't get their hands on her friends, they could use Eva to create their own Ghost Network.

I'm not just the prototype. I'm the raw material.

<73>

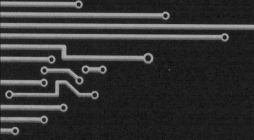

Nine

"Do you think that ancient temple's real?" Akane shut one eye, tilted her head, and wrinkled her nose. "Something about it looks off to me."

"It's about as real as the Trump Taj Mahal in Vegas," scoffed Salome. "That's a fake if ever I saw one. I bet they sprinkle sand on it every morning."

Youssef had halted the Land Rover on a broad patch of hard earth that formed a yard in front of the Temple. The Ghosts scrambled out, stretching their stiff limbs. Morocco might be beautiful, vibrant, and fascinating, thought John, but after awhile they'd all stopped listening to Youssef's cheery narration on the highway. It had grown unbearably hot in the Land Rover. The two girls had started playing games on their PSPs. Slack had fallen asleep, drooling on John's shoulder. John had stared unseeing out of the window, replaying his father's words over and over again in his head. They'd all woken with a start when Youssef announced their arrival.

Together, as they tried to get the blood flowing in their legs once again, the Ghosts stared up at the mighty walls of an

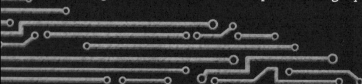

ancient-looking red palace. That dusty golden sunlight encased its walls, making them glow. Its brickwork was decorated with intricate calligraphy and tiling, and the roof was a fantasy combination of high towers, sharp domes, and ornate crenellations. The facade of the temple was marked by lancet and horseshoe arches, and through the biggest of them John could make out a shady courtyard that was also surrounded by a cloister of pointed arches. At least that would be a retreat from the relentless, stifling heat.

"At the absolute earliest, 2012," said Salome firmly. "Look at the mortar between the stones. It's barely dry."

"That's a *bit* of an exaggeration," John scolded her.

"I think it's pretty convincing," said Slack.

"Alaska Boy," grinned Akane. "You've never seen a building older than the Fairbanks Courthouse?"

Slack stuck out his tongue at her.

Youssef was watching them all as he hauled their luggage from the car. "Shall we go inside, then?"

"Sounds good to me," said Slack cheerfully. Picking up his bag, he marched eagerly after Youssef.

"I wonder if they've got a virtual-reality climbing wall?" asked John, catching up with his friend.

"A sliding glass roof, like in a supervillain lair," laughed Salome behind them, as they all strode through the courtyard toward an ornately carved wooden door. "I loved that part of the Wolf's Den."

"I hope it has the fully equipped gym," said Slack wistfully, "with those amazing VR screens."

<75>

"And I *hope* you'll all stop going on about how fabulous the Wolf's Den was," remarked Akane, acerbically. "I didn't get to go there, remember?"

"This'll be just as good," John reassured her. "All the Centers are linked, and they have similar—" He stopped short.

Youssef stepped back from the door and gestured for them to go inside. Even from the Temple's doorway, John could see how different it was from the Wolf's Den.

Maybe that was another disguise, like the faux ancient temple? The passageway looked shabby, with cracked plaster that had been hastily and recently applied. Plain plywood doors led off it, with ordinary Yale locks rather than slick, invisible, electronic systems. Youssef led them past half a dozen of those uninspiring doors. One of them happened to be open, and John caught a glimpse of the interior: a dingy office with utilitarian furniture, a mismatched desk lamp, and a beige rug.

Akane's expression was almost unreadable, thought John as he glanced at her. There was maybe a touch of disappointment there, but he caught the swift smirk of a smile too. Akane had always felt a bit left out because she hadn't been one of the Wolf's Den gang. She must be amused that he, Slack, and Salome were all even more surprised than she was. He couldn't really blame her.

"You'll notice some differences from your previous school," remarked Youssef dryly.

"You're not kidding." Slack's tone was bleak. "Where's the gym?"

"Outside. We call it the desert," laughed Youssef. "You're supposed to toughen up, not build exquisite biceps."

<76>

"I thought they were the same thing," grumbled Slack.

"Toughen up?" asked Salome, raising her eyebrows.

Youssef didn't reply. He turned airily, and they followed him into the central hall: half assembly area, half cafeteria. At least it was lighter here; high open windows let in muted sunlight, and dust motes floated in its beams. But there was no selection of exciting food outlets. There was one serving counter and rows of folding tables with plastic seats attached. The whole place smelled a little musty. Throughout, there was a tang of cement, sawdust, and varnish, as if work had only recently stopped.

"This is . . ." John simply couldn't think of another word. "Different."

"Hmm," said Akane. "You guys led me to expect Google HQ."

"Well, the Wolf's Den kind of *was*," said Salome bleakly.

A woman entered through double swing doors at the far end of the hall and walked toward them, her boot heels clicking on the cement floor. She was tall and lanky, with dark hair pulled back into a long ponytail.

"Hello, and welcome to the Scarab's Temple! I'm Marguerite Lagarde, and I'm the director of this Center."

"Hi. Salome Abraham. It's nice to meet you," said Salome. The others joined in, warily muttering their own names.

"I hope you'll enjoy your time here." Marguerite glanced around and shrugged. "It's a little more basic than what you're used to, I think, but you'll get used to it. And there's plenty of equipment for your training. I'll take you downstairs now. Youssef will make sure your bags are transferred to your rooms." She nodded pleasantly at him.

"What's downstairs?" asked Akane.

<77>

"In the basement we have an extensive network of exascale computers." Marguerite gave an actual, genuine-sounding laugh. "I confess I don't know exactly what those are, but—"

"Exascale computers?" John's eyes lit up. Maybe this place wouldn't be so dreary after all.

"A billion billion calculations per second," grinned Slack. "That's what they are, Ms. Lagarde."

She smiled. "Thanks, Jake. I was told you'd be excited. All I know is that they're brand new, just installed. I'm afraid I don't know much about computers. I do have an iPad. Ha ha!"

All four Ghosts stared at her, then at each other.

A tinge of a blush crept across Marguerite's cheekbones. "I'm not here to be a computer expert, I'm afraid," she said defensively, "so that's one thing I won't be able to help you with. We do have brilliant teachers, I assure you, but I have other skills. I've been an aid worker in combat zones—Libya and Syria, among others—and I'm very knowledgeable about advanced survival. That's what I'm here to help you with."

"Uh," said Salome nervously. "Advanced survival?"

"Suits me, anyway," declared Akane. "Sounds fun!"

"Salome, you know who we're up against," murmured John. "Advanced survival doesn't sound like a bad idea."

"Come with me and I'll show you those lovely computers to cheer you up," said Marguerite, turning toward the double doors. "I know you must be a little disappointed with your surroundings," she went on as she led them down a circular concrete staircase lit by dim wall bulbs. "But the Scarab's Temple is very new, and it was set up quickly, and we've had problems processing the funds from HQ. And . . . well, we don't have the

<78>

cash from multinational tech corporations that the other Centers have access to. Our patron funds this Center from his own resources."

Surprised, John exchanged an apprehensive glance with Slack. His father had provided the resources for this?

The Scarab's Temple might not be the Wolf's Den, but Mikael was pouring everything he had into it. He must be—and then some.

And that meant it might be the most important Center of all.

<79>

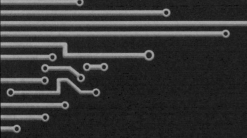

Ten

Outside the Scarab's Temple, the sun was fiercely
intense. John almost recoiled as he stepped out of the shade and
onto the beaten path that led to the sports arena. A hundred feet
away, blurred in the glare, he could make out nimble figures
playing a fast-paced basketball game.

"I want to stay with the 'lovely computers,'" whispered Akane
with a mischievous grin.

"Aw, don't make fun of Marguerite," Slack whispered back,
nudging her. "She's no tech genius, but she's a sweetheart."

"Slack," sighed Salome, "you have to stop falling for everyone
with an XX chromosome."

"And be a bit more skeptical of everybody," muttered John.
"Trust no one."

Slack gave him a surprised glance, but he scooted closer to
Akane too, as if to reassure her that she was the only one for him.
John rolled his eyes.

Another door in the side of the Temple opened with a heavy
creak, and Youssef walked out toward them. He folded his arms
and met each of their curious gazes in turn.

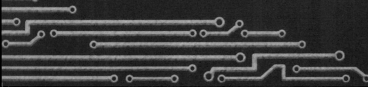

"You've seen the interior? The classrooms, your sleeping areas?"

"Yes," said Salome bleakly.

The classrooms had been small and as dusty and sparse as the dining hall. The bedrooms, despite smelling of fresh paint, had been downright blight. John had thought they felt like prison cells, with their gray blankets and utilitarian sinks, but he reminded himself that looks weren't everything. So long as Lykos was in charge, the stunning Wolf's Den was the true prison.

"Good." Youssef nodded. "It's not luxurious, but the Scarab's Temple is exactly what you four need right now. You'll be safe here to train to the peak of your abilities—in hacking, in self-defense, and in survival. You'll need everything we can teach you if you want to elude your enemies."

"You teach survival?" asked Slack. "As well as driving?"

"Marguerite takes care of extreme survival training," said Youssef dryly. "My specialties are algorithms, data structure, Boolean algebra, and AI."

"Oh." Slack stared at the ground, a blush creeping over his cheekbones and ears.

John almost laughed but managed to stop himself. Since he'd met him, Slack had been acting like Youssef was little more than a cab driver. John felt a little sorry for his friend, but Slack's obvious mortification was pretty funny.

"I'll have a student show you the sports facilities," said Youssef, turning toward the ongoing basketball game. "No fancy virtual-reality screens, but you don't need those to build a high level of fitness—I assure you. At the Scarab's Temple, you'll get all

<81>

the screen time you need in class. Ah! Hello, Collins. Come here for a moment."

The boy who walked toward them was very tall and muscular, his close-cropped head held at an arrogant angle. He stared down his aristocratic nose at Slack with an air of disdain.

"Who are these people?" he asked Youssef.

"New students," Youssef told him. "Make them feel at home, Collins, and show them around the exterior. Introduce them to some of the others."

"Yes, Youssef. It'll be a pleasure." His tone contradicted his words.

Turning on his heels, Collins strode toward the basketball court as the Ghosts hurried after him. Slack shot a look at John and wrinkled his nose.

"He seems nice," he whispered sarcastically.

"I am," said Collins over his shoulder. "And I have great hearing."

"Superhuman," muttered Slack.

Salome was the only one who was easily able to keep pace with Collins. "Where's that accent from?" she asked him.

"Lagos," he replied curtly, "in Nigeria."

"I know where Lagos is," snapped Salome. "I'm from Bahir Dar. *In Ethiopia.*"

John grinned and winked at Slack. If anyone could cut this young prince down to size, it was the equally elegant and aristocratic Salome Abraham. It was impossible to miss the look of surprised respect Collins gave her.

"You're previous Center students?" Collins asked, a little less scornfully.

<82>

"We were at the Wolf's Den in Alaska," Salome told him.

"Except for me," added Akane grumpily.

"Well, I dare say you will learn quickly," Collins told her. Maybe it was that aquiline nose that gave him such a disdainful look, but Akane opened her mouth and shut it again, speechless.

Oh, Collins, thought John. *She'll show you!*

"You enjoy basketball?" asked Collins, stopping beside the court. "I suppose you American boys do."

"So do I," Salome said sharply.

"It's a bit tame for me," snapped Akane, glaring at Collins.

He laughed. "This game isn't tame. Why don't you join in? It's free-for-all. No team number limit."

"I'm on it!" Without a moment's hesitation, Slack raced toward the court, the others following at a more sedate pace. By the time John, Salome, and Akane reached the edge of the court, Slack was right in there, springing valiantly for the ball as the other players ran effortless rings around him.

Salome laughed. "Poor Slack. They might as well be NBA players."

John grinned. Slack's blond hair was already dripping with sweat, and he grimaced as a young Pakistani girl half his size dodged him and aimed for the net. She seemed to almost levitate as she gracefully dropped the ball in for a basket.

"I see what they're doing," John said, trying to feel sorry for Slack. At last he cupped his hands to his mouth and yelled, "Slack! Channel IIDA!"

Slack froze, crouched in the melee. He caught John's eyes, perplexed, then gave a sudden bark of laughter. He remained still for a few moments, closing his eyes as the other players

<83>

ignored him. Then he sprang to his feet, bounced nimbly between two taller boys, and snatched the ball.

"Ha!" said Akane." She turned to Collins, her hostility forgotten. "That's not natural ability, is it? They're all a bit too brilliant."

"What makes you say that?" He narrowed his eyes.

She grinned. "Oh, come on. Did every student here have bad accidents when they were little?"

He stared at her, a bit shocked. Then his eyes softened. "Ah," he murmured. "So you do belong here."

"This is amazing," whispered John to Akane. "Is this a Center just for my dad's . . . guinea pigs?" He couldn't quite suppress an edge of bitterness.

"Looks like it," said Akane, her expression awed. "Look at that Chinese boy go. At least I think he's Chinese?"

Collins nodded, and his face became somber. "Yes. That's Zhou Zhou. He's from Chongqing Province in the southwest."

Slack might be channeling his programming into basketball skills now, but he was still out of his depth with the teams and especially with Zhou. The Chinese boy's face was impassive as he leaped into the air and passed the ball with thoughtless, inhuman precision. It easily passed Slack's reaching hand and was caught by a red-haired boy and netted.

Akane had stopped watching the basketball game; she turned and shaded her eyes as she peered at the top of the Temple. "Who are *they*?"

John followed her gaze. Shimmering in the heat, small figures were racing across the roof, vaulting pinnacles, leapfrogging statuettes, and springing across gaps. As they stared, one of the

<84>

figures paused and stared down curiously, then climbed down rapidly from the roof and ran over to them.

"Are you guys new?" The girl had an English accent that John couldn't quite place. She was long-legged, slender, and athletic looking, and her long, pale hair was pulled back into a ponytail. She gazed inquisitively at the Ghosts.

"Luna is the leader of the parkour gang," Collins told them, by way of introduction. "Is that a bit less 'tame' for you, Akane?"

"It certainly is." Akane grinned at Luna.

Luna returned her smile. "You do parkour? This is great! We don't have nearly enough *proper* athletes here. They're all too obsessed with basketball."

"Hey," objected Collins.

"You know it's true, Collins." Luna turned away with a toss of her ponytail. "Come on, Akane. I'll show you around the best part of the school. The roof!"

Grinning, Akane sprinted after her toward the Temple wall. The two girls began to ascend it, eyeing each other's progress as they confidently reached for outcroppings of carvings to grasp.

John turned back to Collins, who was watching the basketball game again. "You can all channel . . ."

"Our programming? Yes." In a mutter, Collins added, "But none of us quite as well as Zhou."

"He looks, uh . . . focused?" suggested John.

"Zhou is unusual—put it that way. Even among Mikael Laine's experiments, he is . . . shall I say, special?" Collins looked reluctantly admiring. He rubbed his hand across his cropped hair. "Zhou can do anything he likes with a computer."

"So can we," added Salome sharply.

<85>

A smile flickered across Collins's severe mouth. "You mean you can hack any computer," he said. "You can follow any pathway, corrupt any system, and reroute any command. I guarantee Zhou can do it faster, but that's not what I meant. I've seen a laptop move toward him without him touching it, as if he was summoning a dog. And when he's frustrated, I've seen one start to smoke."

John and Salome stared at the Nigerian boy. He gave no indication that he was joking.

"You've seen your sleeping pods," Collins went on. "Basic, right? Zhou's looks like it's been transplanted from your Wolf's Den. He's tricked it out with every imaginable gadget, and it might as well have been styled by some designer from Silicon Valley. I thought *my* parents were wealthy."

"He's spoiled, then." Salome wrinkled her nose.

Collins shook his head. "It isn't like that. Fact is I don't think his family is that rich. But he simply sources what he wants online with barely a thought, and the Scarab's Temple indulges him. I mean, in class the teachers barely bother with him. He's so far ahead of everyone else that he could be from Krypton. He's that different."

John and Salome stared at Zhou, then exchanged a glance. Despite his casually impeccable teamwork, the boy barely seemed to interact with his fellow players. He didn't meet anyone's eye; he simply reached out and took the ball or passed it to another pair of waiting hands. Unlike the others, he didn't yell or shriek with excitement or frustration.

John could almost hear Salome's thought, echoed by his own: *Eva?*

<86>

"There was a girl at the Wolf's Den," John began cautiously. "She was different from the others too. What you might call an early experiment. A little unstable, programming-wise? A bit rough around the edges? And about as communicative as Zhou there."

"'Rough' is not how I'd describe Zhou's programming," laughed Collins. "It's more like Tesla engineering: immaculate, superfast, probably belongs in space." He chuckled again and shook his head.

"And maybe not completely practical in a real-world situation."

<87>

Eleven

Zhou Zhou, thought John as he sat in their first
lecture, was maybe not even intended for real-world situations. It
was like Collins had said: the boy seemed to come from another,
more advanced planet.

The classroom was almost too hot for John to focus. Fans cir-
cled overhead, stirring the dusty air, but it remained oppressively
stuffy. Beside him, Slack kept pushing his sweat-soaked hair out
of his eyes, and his pale skin was flushed. John tried not to think
about the heat, concentrating instead on a beetle that scurried
between the slats of one of the window shutters.

"I apologize about the air-conditioning," said Youssef at the
lectern, "but Salif is making every effort to have it fixed. In the
meantime, I'd be grateful if you could turn *your* energies toward
using your programming to address these equations." He
gestured at the whiteboard behind him. "John Laine, for instance.
We are not here to study entomology."

Embarrassed, John switched his gaze back to the whiteboard.
The equations swam in front of him, and he blinked hard to
try and see them. *Come on, Salif,* he thought, remembering the

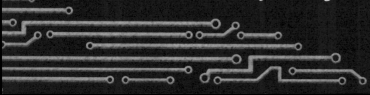

impossibly tall security director he'd met yesterday. *Intimidate those engineers and get this wretched air-conditioning fixed. I bet you can do it with a hard stare . . .*

Youssef's attention was now on two twin girls near the front, so, surreptitiously, John let his gaze slide to Zhou Zhou. The boy sat isolated, entirely by choice, at a scratched wooden desk on the left side of the classroom. Not a bead of sweat had formed on his brow. He barely seemed to move at all, but now and then his fingers would twitch on his keyboard. Then he'd sit back and gaze once more into the middle distance, as if his only discomfort was boredom.

He's not troubled by these Boolean equations at all, John realized, his awe mixed with resentment. *Dad, you could at least have made me a math whiz.*

No doubt he *could* be a math whiz, if he wasn't too hot to channel so much as long division. John suppressed a sigh and pulled his sweaty T-shirt away from his armpits.

"All right," said Youssef sharply from the lectern. He clapped his hands. "This isn't good enough. You need to work faster." His gaze fixed on Slack and John, then Akane and Salome. An amused and rather sadistic smile spread across his lips. "I am aware that some of you have proved you can function in extreme cold. You should be able to keep your wits about you just as well in extreme heat. So, concentrate!"

Blinking, John shook himself. Was that what this was about? Of course, Youssef had told them they were here to learn survival skills along with everything else.

Still, baking them alive in a hot classroom? It felt a little petty.

<89>

"Some of you are a little too smug about your intellectual abilities," smirked Youssef. "Maybe you need to learn more about external environmental factors."

Zhou Zhou had tensed just a little, John noticed. He was staring hard at Youssef, but his eyes seemed strangely bright.

Youssef stalked toward his own laptop, which rested on a desk at the side of the lectern. He reached out to tap a key.

Then Youssef gave a cry of shock and snatched his fingers away. John saw sparks erupt from the keyboard. On the whiteboard behind Youssef, the torturous equations shimmered and jolted.

Then they began to misbehave. Symbols and letters and digits swam into a circle, formed together, and launched into what John could only describe as a barn dance. In and out, rhythmic and playful, twirling around one another until Youssef's carefully planned equations were a chaos of nonsense.

Giggles erupted from the twins at the front. Slack spluttered, and John grinned at him. An Australian boy shouted in surprise, then roared with laughter, pointing.

Zhou Zhou's face was expressionless.

Youssef glared at him, his fists clenched. "Zhou Zhou! What are you doing? Stop immediately!"

There was the tiniest shrug of Zhou's shoulders, but his face didn't even twitch. Akane had turned in her seat to beam at him in amused admiration.

Fuming, Youssef shut his laptop with a slam. "Class is over. I will see you all in ten minutes on the athletics track for punishment circuits." He picked up his laptop and sulked from the room.

<90>

"Worth it," howled Slack, wiping tears of mirth from his eyes. "Worth every circuit, Zhou. Nice one!"

As the students rose in a cheerful clamor and packed up their equipment, John sidled over to Zhou. Sitting down in the chair next to him, he smiled as Zhou calmly packed up.

"That was hilarious," he said, "and brilliant. Can you teach me how to do that?"

For the first time, Zhou met his eyes. The boy's were calm and steady.

"I'm sure I'd be happy to," he said, "but you wouldn't be able to do it."

"I'm pretty quick on the uptake," John assured him. "I know it's a big ask, but—"

"You can't do it," Zhou cut him off. He stood up and stepped away, then turned back.

"And don't be disappointed, John Laine. Be grateful you can't."

<91>

Twelve

She might as well be at a normal high school, Eva thought. A normal high school, with all its boredom, all its frustrations, and all its cliquey, oppressive misery. At least in a normal high school, she could have sneaked out to the mall and soothed her troubled soul with that "retail therapy" she'd heard about. She had never felt so alone in her life as she did now at the Wolf's Den—and that was saying something.

She had never thought she could miss anyone as much as she missed Salome, John, and Slack. *I'm not used to having friends*, she reminded herself. Now that she'd had the experience—and in the most dangerous of circumstances, helping them escape from the Wolf's Den—she found herself terribly lonely without them.

I shouldn't have gotten involved, she thought bitterly. *I never knew friends could make you so unhappy.*

No, Eva reminded herself sharply. She had done the right thing. She was glad she'd helped the Ghosts get out of Roy Lykos's clutches—and if nothing else, his frustrated rage made it all worth it.

I just wish I could see them all again . . .

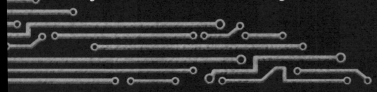

There was no point feeling sorry for herself. Once again, Eva turned her focus to the screen before her. It wasn't as if the teachers took any notice of her in the classroom; ironically, this was the safest place to do her secret research. At the front of the lecture theater, Howard McAuliffe was droning on about she knew not what; her notes were on-screen, and she could easily click back to them if he happened to walk behind her. But her full attention was on the minimized window that she now clicked open. Silently, she worked her own project, hunting the Dark Web for signatures or flares or any trace that her friends might have left in passing. *They're somewhere in the world. I just have to find them.*

At the edge of her mind, she realized McAuliffe was asking for questions. Warily alert, she let part of her attention return to class. Adam Kruz had his hand up to answer a question, and Leo Pallikaris was watching him with starry-eyed adulation as usual. Eva rolled her eyes. Those two had gone unchallenged since the Ghosts had fled; Adam and Leo were top dogs now, with nobody to stand up to them—not even the teachers.

What irritated Eva most at that moment was that Adam's question was a particularly stupid one but Howard McAuliffe was nodding eagerly.

There was no point in raising her hand and saying so. Whenever Eva tried to challenge or dispute a point, the teacher would shoot her down immediately. *Especially,* when the teacher concerned was Roy Lykos. But McAuliffe knew who paid his salary too, Eva thought resentfully. Suppressing her urge to laugh in scorn, she sat in silence as Adam made the tritest intervention in the history of computing science.

<93>

The other students were nodding obsequiously, and Eva restricted herself to another roll of her eyes. Then she saw Leo glance over his shoulder with a smirk and tap his keyboard.

At once, the headache struck. With a gasp, Eva gripped her temples.

The headaches were worse than migraines: racking, blinding spasms that left her incapable for long minutes. The screen in front of her blurred into nonsense, and she just managed to minimize her search window before the pain overcame her.

By the time she recovered, she was alone in the classroom; the tutorial was over. Rising unsteadily to her feet, she slapped the Perspex work desk in fury, sending another twinge of pain between her temples. But she was still sane, still thinking straight. The headache was slowly reduced to a dull throb.

Adam and Leo had the malevolence to do this to her—but they didn't have the capability. This, she knew, came from higher up. It was nothing more than a blatant threat; they were letting her know what they could do to her if she didn't cooperate. That was the only possible motive. Somehow, Lykos and Yamamoto *had* managed to get inside her head. Adam and Leo were tools, but not unwitting ones. Eva clenched her teeth as the pain finally subsided.

The silence in the classroom felt oppressively heavy. Although not as oppressive as her rage. *I will defeat you, Roy Lykos*, she thought. *I will. You and your obsequious little pets.*

Sitting down again, Eva pulled her laptop toward her. They had her at their mercy, and they thought she was powerless. That was why they were punishing her so blatantly.

<94>

Well, they'd made one fundamental miscalculation: they'd underestimated her. Somehow, it seemed, Lykos had gotten access to her programming.

Maybe he'd forgotten that doors opened two ways.

Remembering all that John had told her about Akane Maezono, Eva closed her eyes. It wasn't proper meditation, but it was enough: she knew by now how to look inside herself. And inside Eva, there was a lot more than unresolved family issues.

Her programming was confused, and it was missing parts; it was blank where whole lines of code should be, but it was accessible if you knew how—and Eva knew *how* better than anyone. Roy had accessed her via the mainframe computer, and that meant that somewhere, he'd left an imprint of his access key. The door, she told herself again, opened both ways.

Her eyes still closed, Eva's fingertips strayed to her keyboard. *You and me, laptop. Between us we'll find his access key.*

Leaving Eva alone and friendless: that had been their big mistake. Nobody cared about her headaches. Nobody cared that she sat here alone in the lecture theater, literally left to her own devices.

Eva smiled. She tapped a command. She tapped another. She let her eyes flicker open.

I've got you, Roy Lykos.

In retrospect, the access key was the easy part. Now her search began—and her search had to cover cyberspace. She might

<95>

as well have been flying through real space in search of some elusive, capricious comet that kept changing its path.

But all she needed was time, she reminded herself. And she had nothing but that.

Nobody would know she'd been here. Her route through cyberspace was too random, too chaotic, and too well camouflaged. There was *no way* anyone could know she'd made this search, she reassured herself.

Eva glanced back cautiously at every cyberspace pathway as she left it. No, she was sure. No one knew she was here. She'd imagined that mark on a tiny planet, that swirl of disturbance in a nebula, that notch on the edge of a black hole.

The lights were dimming. Maybe it was the electricity; maybe it was her own exhaustion.

Eva closed her laptop.

<96>

Thirteen

A mark on a tiny planet, a swirl of disturbance in
a nebula . . .

Salome jolted out of her reverie. Had she fallen asleep? She
didn't think so. She couldn't have, because her feet were still
working the pedals of the rather primitive exercise bike. Her
brain had been miles away, and then a sudden notion smashed
into her thoughts out of nowhere.

Stepping off the bike and toweling the sweat from her face
and arms, she frowned. *A mark on a tiny planet* . . . It had been
less of a coherent thought, more of a dreamlike vision. And,
somehow, yet again, she found her thoughts turning to Eva
Vygotsky.

It wasn't surprising, really. John and Slack had taken to the
Scarab's Temple like ducks to particularly enticing water, and they
seemed to have barely any time for her anymore. The friction
between the two boys and Collins was lessening every day, and
they actually seemed to enjoy the tall Nigerian's company.

As for Akane, she might have been made for the basic,
outdoorsy environment of the Temple. She and Luna—whose

unfamiliar accent turned out to be Cornish—had been instant soul mates. Akane spent every spare minute with the parkour gang, conquering the Temple's highest reaches and surfing the slopes of the dunes. Salome sensed that Akane had been glad to find her own friends—friends who didn't have a Wolf's Den history—and she'd been almost too eager to detach herself from John, Slack, and Salome.

Salome was glad her friends were enjoying themselves, but she couldn't help feeling a twinge of sadness. She had never had many close friends her own age; drifting around the world after her diplomat father and frequent changes of school had made that impossible. Why else would she have so enjoyed the company of that small gang of thieves she'd fallen in with at her school in Hamburg? They'd been rich kids, but they'd been bored, and their campaign of petty and not-so-petty thefts had given them all a thrill of transgression and a bond that had been closer than family. She didn't know what had come over her—a touch of rebellion, maybe, or just a longing for a tight friendship group and her own secrets?—and inevitably their crimes had come to light. Salome had been lucky not to be expelled with the rest. She still felt a pang of survivor guilt about that, but their all-for-one-and-one-for-all conspiracy hadn't been healthy—she knew that now.

In the last term at the Wolf's Den she had been surprised and delighted to find such unexpected soul mates in the other Ghosts. Their bond had been faster and closer and based on something a little more noble, a lot more in line with Salome's image of herself.

<98>

Now, since they'd come to the Scarab's Temple, it seemed as if their small gang was drifting apart, just as they were getting to know one another. On the other hand, Salome couldn't really blame Akane for looking for friends beyond the Ghost Network. Maybe they *did* talk a bit too much about the Wolf's Den. It was hard not to—but Salome missed Akane.

Unsurprisingly, though, it was Eva she missed most of all.

Eva had always been her friend. At least, Salome had started trying to become Eva's friend from the moment she'd arrived at the Wolf's Den. The silent, strange girl had fascinated Salome from the very first moment, and Eva had seemed so *alone*. It was true she'd wanted it that way—abandoned on the trans-Siberian railway with no memory of any family or history, Eva had been the most self-contained person Salome had ever met.

But Salome knew how to look beneath the surface. She knew Eva's reserve masked a deep well of need and loneliness—and Salome Abraham wasn't about to let that go unchallenged. She'd always had plans to save the world, Salome remembered with a wry smile, but she'd known she must first start with Eva.

Since her arrival at the Scarab's Temple, Salome scolded herself, she'd waited way too long to start properly worrying about Eva. Quickly, she wiped down the bike and headed for the showers. (*And how could the showers in the Sahara be this cold?* she asked herself with a shiver as she stepped under the water.)

It was as if all her repressed concern for Eva had coalesced in an instant into near panic. *What have I been thinking?*

The Ghosts had been at the Scarab's Temple for a few weeks, and this Center had been no less intensively busy for its students than the Wolf's Den—but that was no excuse. Eva was *vulnerable*.

<99>

That fanciful thought about planets and nebulas, crashing into Salome's head as she exercised—it had been her guilty conscience fighting to be seen, Salome was sure of it. Eva might as well be lost in space for all the thought Salome had given her!

Salome scrubbed herself quickly and stepped out of the chilly shower. Dressing swiftly and tossing her gym clothes into the laundry, she hurried for her "pod," as Collins insisted on calling the compact and basic sleeping quarters she shared with Akane.

Eva was too vulnerable to be left to the mercies of Roy Lykos and his cronies. Yes, Salome had promised with the others that she'd make no attempt to contact the outside world or even the Centers' intranet. Yes, she'd been warned by Mikael, and she knew it was dangerous.

But if the Ghosts themselves were in danger, how much peril must Eva be in? The Russian girl was still in the Wolf's Den—figuratively and literally. The Ghosts had sworn to go back for her, and they *hadn't*.

A mission was one thing—but loyalty to friends was important too. Maybe more so. She might be one of Mikael's Ghosts, but she was also Salome Abraham, and she should never forget that. And—at least since that horrible time in Hamburg—Salome Abraham would *never* abandon a friend.

Salome flipped open her laptop so fast she almost knocked it off the desk. Grimly, she logged on and clicked quickly through to the deeper channels of the internet, the ones the Ghosts had fruitlessly searched on many occasions for information about themselves. If Eva had been anywhere online, Salome knew, she'd have been here.

<100>

The room was completely quiet except for the soft clicking of Salome's keyboard and her slightly rapid breathing. What was she looking for? She didn't even know. She could only sink herself in the dark recesses of cyberspace, hunting for a sign.

A mark, a disturbance, a notch.

Then, out of the corner of her eye, she caught sight of it: not a swirling cloud of stars in a nebula and not a kink in the orbit of a planet . . . she wasn't really in space, after all.

But that was what it felt like, when she noticed the flare.

Salome took a deep breath, her hands trembling above the keyboard. *Eva.*

Her natural caution taking over, Salome stared at it for a very long time. Then, slowly and deliberately, she clicked and acknowledged the flare.

Contact.

Her eyes widened, and her heart plummeted. The return contact had been sent. But she shouldn't have seen that flicker of activity in the corner of the screen, not yet.

Because that was not Eva.

It had been barely visible, almost undetectable, a tiny echo response that was gone in an instant. But Salome saw and heard it as clearly as a suspicious click on a landline.

What was that? Her gut went cold. *Did somebody just copy my location?*

Leaping out of her chair, Salome snatched at the laptop's cables, yanking them out of the wall. She thumbed the off switch hard, and the screen went black. Her heart thrashed in her chest. *How could I have been so stupid?*

<101>

Standing trembling in front of her desk, Salome felt her chest constrict as she tried to breathe. *Somebody copied my location. Our location!*

But she'd had to do it, she reminded herself. The urge to find Eva had been irresistible, and it had come from the deepest part of Salome, the part her programming couldn't touch.

Hadn't it?

Shutting her eyes, Salome breathed deeply in and out until her heartbeat began to steady.

It wasn't a disaster. It *couldn't* be a disaster. She wouldn't allow it to be.

Everything would be fine. She knew Eva was out there now, and Eva would know that she knew. That was what mattered. That distant alert at Salome's tentative acknowledgment of the flare—it had been so fleeting, gone in less than an instant.

It had been some automatic computer response. It *couldn't* matter.

Eva was what mattered. Clenching and unclenching her fists, Salome calmed herself.

She wouldn't tell anyone what she'd done. She'd carry on as if nothing had happened.

Because nothing would. *Nothing* would.

<102>

Fourteen

Roy Lykos micromanaged his world. Everything he did
was deliberate, and everything he did was under his own control.
Everything his staff and students did was under his direction
too. He had structured his environment very carefully to ensure
that he was never surprised, never taken aback, and never caught
off guard. When it happened, it shook something at Roy's very
core. The Ghosts had done it to him when they fled the Wolf's
Den and escaped across the frozen wastes of Alaska, and their
defiance had sent him into a rage that had shocked even him.

When a glitch entered his meticulously crafted systems, it
was not something he didn't notice. It was never something that
didn't matter. Roy Lykos never, ever did a double take.

He did one now.

Taking a breath, he went still. He watched his screen, waiting
for a repetition. It didn't come.

That didn't mean the first time hadn't mattered.

"Yasuo," he said.

"What is it, Roy?" Yasuo Yamamoto was not a man to hurry
or panic, but his attention was instantly on Lykos. He stood over

him, and Lykos could almost feel the bristling of Yamamoto's nerves beneath his skin. Yasuo was the colleague he needed: a serenely patient man who knew when to be concerned. Roy was glad he'd recruited the man early for his cause.

Lykos sat back, gesturing at the screen. "My access key to the mainframe. It was used recently."

"That's unexpected." Yamamoto's calm voice held an electric undercurrent.

"Indeed. It appears I took three attempts to log in. It appears I didn't remember my password."

"That doesn't happen," said Yasuo matter-of-factly.

"Indeed." Roy Lykos leaned forward, studying the screen with poisonous fascination.

"Then we should track the attempts." Yamamoto smiled.

"I already did." Lykos gave a sigh that contained a mix of patience and seething malevolence. He felt both, after all. "It's as if they don't realize I'm some sort of coding genius. I followed the intruder. Left a flare behind her, to see if it would hook any little fish."

Yamamoto laughed. "Her?"

"Oh, we know who it was, Yasuo." Lykos laid his fingers on the keyboard like a piano maestro pausing before a concerto. With a deep, satisfying breath, he began to type, his fingertips flowing over the keys. He didn't even have to think about which to touch; he might not be some programmed teenage cyborg, but it came to him now like breathing or sleeping. Who did those brats imagine they were dealing with?

"Like bear prints in fresh snow," he murmured. "Poor Eva. And she thought she was being so subtle."

<104>

Yamamoto smiled, intent on the screen. "I see it."

"Yes." Lykos sat back, cracking his knuckles. "They thought my flare was Eva's. Contact has been made."

Yamamoto leaned closer over his shoulder. "They responded to your flare? Are they fools?"

"Yes. Or one of them is." Lykos laughed, linking his fingers and stretching his arms above his head. "Look at that location pin."

Yasuo slapped him on the shoulder. "Excellent."

The human touch was a little surprising, but Lykos found he didn't mind, just this once. It was a time for mild celebration.

"The Ghost Network has been good to us, Yasuo. Let's take a moment to appreciate that kindness."

"Shouldn't we strike fast?" Yasuo made a face. "No wolf ever caught a rabbit by giving it a head start."

"There's no hurry, my friend. The Ghosts are not going anywhere, and we have plenty of time to pick them off in their new location." Lykos smiled up at his colleague.

"After all, one of them has just told us exactly where that is . . ."

<105>

Fifteen

Nothing had happened. Everything was quiet and normal, or as quiet and normal as it could ever be at a Center. Salome was torn between relief and the constant, nagging torment of waiting for an explosion.

The truth was she couldn't quite believe she'd gotten away with it.

Classes continued, day after intense day, with a mercifully repaired air-conditioning system (or perhaps, John suggested, it had never been broken in the first place). Survival training was a pain in the programming butt, with Marguerite every bit as strict and unforgiving as Youssef was with classroom errors. Youssef hadn't been quite straightforward when he said the only gym was the desert; there was one, but it was basic and Spartan. All the same, it was a blissful retreat, where the Ghosts could train at their own unrelenting pace—and then discover that they still weren't quite fit enough for Marguerite's stringent demands. There was remarkably little time for PSPs and Steam gaming, but Slack and John always seemed to make some.

The excursions, though hard work, were the part of the curric-
ulum Salome looked forward to most. Who could have imagined
that a seemingly monotonous expanse like the Sahara desert
could be so changeably beautiful?

On their sixth Monday at the Scarab's Temple, Salome woke
with a far lighter heart than she had had for weeks. *Nothing has
happened*, she repeated in her head, her usual morning mantra
now. It was a new week, a new week without a threatening
incident or contact from Lykos. And what was more, the school
had planned an expedition far into the desert.

"On camels!" Akane must have woken at the same moment.
She threw off her sheet and leaped out of bed, grinning. "Hey,
Salome, wake up! Exped day!"

"I am awake," said Salome, rubbing her eyes. "Why *are* you so
perky in the morning?"

"It's my natural exuberance. Come on! There's gonna be a
barbecue. Games. And we're camping overnight." Akane's eyes
shone.

"I know all that. Give me five more minutes . . ."

"No, absolutely not! Get showered and dressed and we'll go
wake the boys!"

"Oh, all right. After all, I cannot wait till Slack encounters a
camel," laughed Salome, capitulating. She grabbed her towel and
toiletry bag. "He'll finally meet his match."

For once, the boys were already up and dressed; it seemed
John and Slack were as thrilled about the expedition as Salome
and Akane. John, thought Salome, had grown more confident
and more relaxed as the weeks went by; he seemed far happier, as
if the Scarab's Temple suited him despite its austere conditions.

<107>

"You like this place," she said to him when they had finished breakfast, gathered their packs, and were making their way out to the broad square in front of the Temple.

"I do," John agreed quietly. Akane and Slack were striding ahead through the courtyard, gabbing about camels with Collins and Luna; it was rare and rather nice to talk to John privately, Salome realized.

"It feels like . . ." Salome hesitated. "It feels more like your dad here, you know? I know the Wolf's Den was his creation too, but this is more so. Essence of Mikael, you know what I mean?"

"I know exactly what you mean." John smiled at her. "I'm still mad at him, but I can't bring myself to be . . . really mad at him."

"I understand," she murmured. "Your dad's put you through some tough times, John, but he's never stopped loving you."

"I know." He smiled again, not quite meeting her eyes. Then he turned to stare ahead to the outer square, and his eyes widened. "Look! Our noble charges!"

They both gazed at the beasts, who squatted on the ground, their liquid eyes fixed on their potential riders with a light of malicious mischief. Salome swallowed hard.

"This is going to be fun." She blurted a nervous laugh.

Slack, of course, was first to approach his camel—which lightened Salome's mood yet again. There was a lot of snapping, glaring, and braying objection—"Some of it from the camel," she pointed out to John, wiping tears of mirth from her eyes.

Her own camel was a lot more placid and cooperative, Salome was relieved to find, and it was still cool early morning by the time the students were swaying out on camelback onto one of the tracks that led toward the distant dunes. It was so relaxing

<108>

that Salome found herself almost forgetting her blunder with Eva's flare. It seemed so very much part of the past. With the soothing, rocking motion of the camel, its pungent musky odor filling her nostrils, and the rising sun gilding the dunes, it was easy to believe that nothing mattered but the moment.

By lunchtime, the small caravan had arrived at their camping site, where a vast white tent had already been erected, its canvas sides rolled up. From a distance, Salome could smell the charcoal tang of a smoking barbecue, and her stomach growled.

"That smells *good!*" exclaimed Slack.

"The meat isn't even cooking yet," laughed Akane.

Slack thumped his chest. "Smoke mean fire," he growled. "Fire mean cooking. Cooking mean meat."

Collins rolled his eyes, and Luna grinned. "Slack, you can't be a caveman when somebody else is feeding you. Go kill an antelope or something."

"Me go kill food," drawled Slack solemnly as, with Salif's amused assistance, he clambered awkwardly from his long-suffering camel. "Or me go play cricket. One or the other."

John punched him affectionately. "You barely know what cricket is."

"Cricket like baseball, only more civilized." Slack thumped his chest again. "Like me."

It was hard to bowl, bat, or field properly when Slack seemed willing to keep up his caveman persona indefinitely. Salome was in helpless fits much of the time along with the others. Just as well, she thought, since it kept their minds off the barbecue; the smells drifting from it were by now almost irresistible, spicy and tangy.

<109>

There was only one member of the party who wasn't engaged with the cricket match, Salome realized: Zhou, of course. He sat under a makeshift shelter of shawls and throws on poles, engrossed in a *Cyborg* graphic novel.

"Hey, Zhou!" called Collins after a few overs. "Come and join my team; we're losing without you!"

Zhou ignored him and turned a page.

The others exchanged exasperated glances, but only Slack decided to do something about it. Hunching his shoulders and dragging his fists, he stomped over to stand in front of the boy. He'd have been throwing shade, thought Salome, if Zhou wasn't comfortably ensconced in it already.

"You play cricket," demanded Slack in his caveman voice. "You hold bat. Hit ball."

Zhou ignored him even more thoroughly than he'd ignored Collins, if that was even possible.

"Bat," thundered Slack again. "Bat you hold in paw. Ball you thwack."

Zhou turned another page.

Sulking like a true caveman, Slack plodded back to the game. It was only minutes later that Collins hit a six, and as his team roared their approval, the ball rolled to a stop at Zhou's feet.

"Hey, Zhou!" yelled a triumphant Collins. "Throw that back, will you?"

"Yeah, come on, Zhou!" called Salif from the mid-on position. "Get involved!"

"Zhou chuck ball," bellowed Slack, crashing his fists together.

A chorus of voices agreed, but Zhou simply focused on his comic book.

<110>

"I'll get it," called Luna, and began to jog toward Zhou.

But Slack clearly couldn't take it anymore. "Stop being a jerk, Zhou," he yelled angrily, breaking character. "Luna, don't encourage him. He's acting out like a four-year-old."

For the first time, Zhou reacted. Setting down his book, he rose gracefully to his feet, lifted the ball, and threw it.

It was impossible to follow its arc. The first any of them really saw of it was when it smashed into Collins's wicket, causing Collins to leap away from the crease to dodge the ball. He blinked in shock as the ball broke a stump and sent the bails flying.

The ball rolled to a halt; Salome was surprised it wasn't smoking.

"Out?" called Salome nervously.

Collins shrugged and walked.

"A man of honor," called Slack, then muttered something to John. Salome edged closer to join the conversation.

John nodded to her. "Slack was just saying that was unfair."

"I know." Salome bit her lip. "I shouldn't have called 'out,' but the atmosphere—"

"It's not your fault," said Slack. "That's not what I mean. It's only a fun game anyway. It's just that I bet *Zhou* wouldn't have walked in that situation."

"To be fair, he wouldn't ever be in that situation," Salome pointed out.

"True," said John, "and let's talk about the main thing here. Did you *see* that throw?"

"Like Cyborg himself was pitching," said Slack with reluctant admiration. "How did he do it? Because I don't think it was a lucky strike."

<111>

"No, and that thing in class—remember?" John shook his head. "How did he get Youssef's computer to misbehave so entertainingly? I've never seen anything like it, and Zhou barely touched his keyboard—I was sitting near him."

"I wish I could ask him," said Slack, "though I'm not sure I like him."

"I did ask him," said John. "And he said, 'You wouldn't be able to do it. And you should be grateful you can't.'"

"The cheeky jerk," said Slack darkly.

"Maybe, but I'm pretty sure he's right." John shrugged.

"Slack, you're *not sure you like Zhou?*" said Salome severely. "You can't stand him! Just admit it."

Slack shrugged and grinned. "You got me. Anyway, look, they're starting to serve the food. And I'm *starving.*"

"That's news?" Salome winked at him, and they walked off the makeshift cricket field with the rest of the teams.

The barbecue was sizzling and smoking. Succulent lamb kebabs, chicken, and roasted peppers sent fumes of deliciousness drifting their way while Salif handed out steaming crispy slices of the sweet pigeon pie called pastille. Just as in Casablanca, the air was filled with the scents of cinnamon and cumin, ginger and allspice. John sniffed the air, and his stomach growled audibly.

"I'm going to ask Zhou right now how he does it," said Slack, grabbing a burger that was dripping with harissa.

"I'm not sure that's a good—" began Salome, but she fell silent. Slack was already approaching Zhou.

"Hey, Zhou, that's some overarm technique," grinned Slack. "You want to teach me how, or is that another thing we should all be grateful we can't do?"

<112>

Maybe Slack was expecting to be ignored again, but it didn't happen this time. Zhou turned, his cheekbones darkening with rage.

"Are you mocking me, *dude*? Are you? Bring it, as you American idiots say!"

"Hey! Hey!" Slack backed off, raising his hands, one of which still clutched the burger. "No need to get so aggressive. I just asked a question!"

"Maybe you and your friends should ask fewer questions," snarled Zhou, shooting a hostile glance at John.

Slack's temper snapped. "And maybe you should get off your high horse and quit thinking you're better than all of us. You freak!"

"Hey, steady, Slack," Salome said nervously, sensing a tipping point coming.

"Freak?" growled Zhou, an edge of danger to his voice. "What does that make you? All of you?"

"Yeah, 'cause we're all here for the same reason," yelled Slack. "Even if nobody likes to talk about it—that's what brought us here." Marguerite Lagarde was hurrying toward him, a look of alarm on her face, but Slack ignored her. "And you're no smarter than any of us, Zhou—you just like to think you are."

"I don't *like* to think anything," snapped Zhou. "I just know it!"

"Oh, yeah?" Slack's face had turned deep red. "Go on, then! Prove you're Superman!" He shoved the boy's shoulder, not too hard but tauntingly. "*Prove it!*"

There was a hideous silence for all of three seconds. Marguerite had come to a halt, frozen, her eyes panicked. Salif had begun to run toward Zhou, but it was too late.

<113>

The boy spun on his heels and glared hard at the barbecue gas tanks. For a fraction of a second there was an even heavier silence, if that was possible: a deadening of the air.

Then the gas tanks exploded.

Sand erupted, volcanically. A ball of flame billowed and blossomed into a great orange ball; only then did the sound hit Salome's ears. She ducked for cover with the rest. Fleeing, Salome cowered with John behind a stack of chairs, her hands over her ears.

The pressure wave and the deafening boom faded, leaving an eerie stillness in its wake. A girl screamed, more in anger than fear, Salome realized.

Marguerite was on her feet again, running toward the barbecue. "Was anyone hurt?" she yelled. "Is everyone OK?"

"Everyone's fine," Salif staggered a little as he rose. He looked shaken and angry but oddly unsurprised. The barbecue nearby was a tangled mess of destroyed metal. "Everyone take your food. Chefs, wander your way back to the vehicles." He turned to glare at Zhou with an absolutely murderous expression.

"You go too far, boy," Salif growled, taking a menacing step toward Zhou. His eyes were as hard and cold as diamonds, Salome noticed with surprise; she respected Salif, but she'd never thought of him as potentially dangerous. A small shiver went through her bones.

"Zhou Zhou!" shouted Marguerite, marching toward the boy. Her face was white with fury; she looked as if she wanted to grab Zhou and shake him, but she stopped right in front of him instead, clenching her fists. "You know this is unacceptable. Get in the jeep right now. You're going back to the Center. I wish

<114>

I could expel you, but you're confined to your pod till further notice. Till I hear from the—the patron." Marguerite gulped with fury, taking a breath. "Do you hear me? *Get in the jeep!*"

Without a single word or argument, Zhou strode away with Salif toward the parked vehicles. Behind him, the other students were gabbing animatedly, their voices raised high in anger and disbelief and, in one or two cases, awe.

One of those was Slack. He spat out sand. "What the heck just happened?"

"You managed to provoke quite a reaction," snapped Salome. Her hands were still shaking. "Great result, Slack."

"Hey, it wasn't my fault," he retorted.

"He's at the point of being expelled! He's done something awful, Slack, but you had no need to provoke him."

"He barely needs provoking," barked Slack. "He's dangerous. I'm glad he's out!" His expression grew distant again, and a little nervous. "I mean, did you see *that?*"

John shook his head. He looked dumbfounded: a fair enough reaction, thought Salome. She didn't know what to think herself.

"I'm going to call it," said John. "Slack, Zhou's right. I couldn't do the things he does. And I *am really* glad about that."

<115>

Sixteen

Early sunlight woke Salome; she yawned and stretched, then curled under the covers, pulling a sheet over her head.

"Five more minutes," she mumbled.

"Whom are you talking to?" Akane, of course, was sitting up on her camp bed. "I don't think anyone else is awake yet. It's quiet out there."

Salome blinked and struggled to sit up on her own camp bed. Dawn glowed on the thick white canvas of the tent sides. No shadows moved outside.

Akane was right; they must be the first ones up. But surely the expedition would leave early to get back to the Scarab's Temple? It was soon going to get really hot out in the dunes.

As Salome swung her legs off the bed, the events of the previous day came back to her in a rush. In the cool light of day, it seemed scarcely believable. *Zhou exploded the gas tanks. With his mind.*

With luck, Salome told herself, *that* was the explosion she had been waiting for. A literal one. Nothing else was going to happen.

Her online acknowledgment of the mysterious flare had gone unnoticed. They were safe.

Salome shoved the memory of Zhou's parlor trick aside and with it her worries about Lykos and the flare. "We should go and see who's awake. I really think they wanted to get going earlier than this. What are Salif and Marguerite thinking?"

Akane crawled to the flap of their two-person tent and pushed it aside. She seemed to stay there for a long time, then poked her head outside.

"Well?" said Salome impatiently.

"I don't know what Salif and Marguerite are thinking," whispered Akane. "And there's no way of finding out. They're gone."

"Gone? What do you mean, 'gone'?"

Akane twisted her head. "What does 'gone' usually mean, Salome?"

Salome darted to the flap and shoved her head outside. Her heartbeat was already quickening, and when she stumbled out into the deserted camp, it went into overdrive.

"They're *all* gone!" she cried in disbelief.

Across the huge flat area outside their tent, where they had all eaten barbecue and played cricket, there were nothing but scuff marks and confused footprints. The massive tent with open sides was gone; not even a tent pole remained. Most of the other smaller sleeping tents were also gone. Vehicle tracks scored the hard sand, marking reverses and turns. There were camel footprints and lumps of camel dung, but no camels. A blackened scorch mark on the ground, like a Rorschach inkblot, was the only evidence that a gas barbecue had exploded here.

<117>

Beyond the camp area, the dunes glowed cinnamon-red in the light that spilled over the purple and golden horizon. The sandhills receded into the unseeable distance for miles, their slopes rising and falling like ocean waves.

Only one tent remained. Salome ran to it, ripping the flaps open.

"John! Slack! Wake up! We've been abandoned!"

As the two boys crawled sluggishly from their beds, rubbing their eyes and muttering in disbelief, Salome turned to stare at the desert again. Was this something to do with Lykos? Had her blunder caught up with her after all?

"This . . . this is . . . what do they think they're doing?" John stood shocked and immobile, fully awake at last.

"What the heck?" barked Slack.

"This makes no sense." Salome bit her nails. "Do you think . . . do you think this was deliberate?"

"Who knows what goes through those guys' heads?" said Akane grimly. "All I know is that we have to get back to the Center, whether they want us there or not. We can't stay out in the desert all day."

"Do you think something happened to the others?" Salome felt like crying, but she held her jaw firm as she thought, *This is my fault. I brought this on us.*

"Were they attacked? Abducted?"

"Surely we'd have heard something?" Akane didn't sound all that sure, though.

"And why would they leave just us?" Slack shrugged. "It doesn't make sense."

"Yes. It does." John gave a growl of frustration. "They're testing us. Don't you see?"

<118>

The others stared at him. "No way," said Slack.

"Why just us?" Akane spread out her hands.

"Because we're newbies. Noobs. That's why." John looked furious. "It's a stupid, stupid *test*."

They stared at one another, their stomachs plummeting. "They get to endanger the students for a *test*?" demanded Akane. "Was this what it was like at the Wolf's Den? Because if so, I'm glad I never went there." She glowered.

"I don't know if they *get to*," growled John. "I don't know if even my dad would be this reckless. But Marguerite's like the worst drill sergeant ever, for all her nicey-nicey front. She loves to tell us we're soft, she loves saying things like, 'This isn't like Syria or Yemen; toughen up.' And Youssef would love this because he's a sadist anyway. Remember all those punishment circuits?"

"Yes, but Salif wouldn't let them," said Akane.

"Salif obviously did," Slack pointed out. "He does what he's told. He's head of security, not the whole school."

"And I'm not so sure about Salif," muttered Salome. "There's something unnerving about him."

"Whatever's happened, Akane's right. We *have* to get back to the Scarab's Temple," said John, clenching his fists.

"But how do we do that?" Salome spread her hands. She looked on the verge of tears. "We don't know enough about desert survival. Not yet."

"We know a bit," said Slack reassuringly. "At least Marguerite taught us that. We know we need to start as soon as possible, for one thing. How far did we travel yesterday?"

"Did we bother to measure it?" said Akane bleakly. "I was too busy watching the scenery."

<119>

"I've a feeling we'll get *very* tired of the scenery before today's over," said John.

"I don't even know which direction to go!" exclaimed Salome. "There are tracks, but they're muddled. They go off in several directions—look." She turned around in a circle, pointing. Tire tracks and camel poop alike led off in every direction. "I heard quite a bit of wind last night. The dune sand is much softer, and it'll have drifted. I doubt there are any useful tracks at all."

Slack, ever practical, was already dismantling and packing up one of the tents. He displayed a grimace of annoyance, but he didn't look scared. "I know the direction," he said, stuffing a tent carelessly into its roll.

"You do?" John blinked. "How?"

"Don't ask me." Slack paused in his angry packing and stared up at the sky. "The stars might be almost gone, but I have a map." He tapped his temple.

The other three stared at him. "I didn't know you of all people were keeping track yesterday," said Akane skeptically.

"I wasn't." He shrugged. "I can see it. That's all. I can see the stars' position relative to the sunrise. It's like a—" He fell silent abruptly and bit his lip. "It's like a diagram in my brain. Clear as a Google Map."

"IIDA," laughed Akane suddenly. "Thank you, 'Mom.'"

John grinned. "We can do this. Let's not panic. Focus on our programming and we'll make it."

"Wait." Akane's eyes grew unfocused. "I've got an idea."

"What?" asked John. But Akane was already sitting down, cross-legged on the sand, her eyes beatifically closed.

"Is she meditating?" asked Slack.

<120>

"Sh!" commanded Salome.

Akane was silent for a very long time; only the tips of her fingers twitched slightly. At last she blinked her eyes wide open.

"I knew I remembered something," she said triumphantly, springing to her feet. She darted to the burned patch where the barbecue had been and crouched to dig in the blackened sand with her hands. The others stared.

Then she jumped up, brandishing a metal canister. "Water!" she exclaimed. "I knew there were flasks left beside the barbecue. This one got buried in the blast. Or they left it there deliberately. Maybe they're not completely irresponsible."

The others ran to her side. "Not a lot of water," pointed out Salome. "A gallon. Are you sure there's no more?"

Akane crouched and dug again. After a while she rose, dusting her hands. "No. We have a quarter of a liter each. I'm *sure* there was more. Maybe they were destroyed in the explosion?"

"Or Marguerite took it when they left," growled John.

"Or Salif," added Salome.

"It'll have to be enough." Slack shrugged.

"We'll ration it," said John. "But that means the sooner we start, the better. The temperature's cool enough right now, but it won't stay that way for long."

"We're not going to make it," said Salome, her voice trembling. "What the—*oh my God!*"

She shrieked and danced sideways, almost stumbling, as a scorpion scuttled out of the churned-up sand where the barbecue had been. It fled before Slack could stomp on it.

"Snakes. Scorpions." Akane shivered. "Even parkour doesn't cover this stuff."

<121>

"Snakes." Slack went pale. "I hadn't thought of that."

"Just stay alert," said John, though fear churned in his gut. "Let's keep our eyes open. I don't feel like doing anything Marguerite said, but I guess her survival advice is sound."

"Do they even care if we make it back?" asked Slack grimly. "Maybe if we're not tough enough, we're expendable."

Akane straightened, her eyes flashing. "We're tough enough," she said firmly. "We can't let this beat us. We can't let *them* beat us."

Slack nodded, slowly at first but then rapidly. "You're right," he declared. "Akane? I wish you *had* been at the Wolf's Den. We'd have gotten along better with you there."

"Hear, hear," agreed Salome, with a smile toward Akane. "We'd have been a team even then. And we're going to be a team right now."

Akane blushed and stirred the sand with her foot. But she looked pleased.

"Right," said John, balancing the water bottle in his palm. "Let's get started. We'll show these guys what the Ghost Network is made of."

"We'd better," said Salome quietly, glancing at the rising sun. "Because if we don't, we're in really big trouble."

They had only the tents they'd slept in, the water bottle, and their own packs, so it didn't take long to get organized. Slack led the way, heading confidently toward the brightest part of the horizon just as a dazzling glare spilled over it.

"You know Slack's navigation will only take us so far?" whispered Akane to Salome. "He's going by the stars. That's fine for

<122>

a rough direction, but, eventually, we'll need something more precise."

"We'll cross that dune when we come to it." Salome said quietly. "All we can do right now is walk."

She had never been so thirsty. John was far stricter about the water than Salome had imagined he could be, but even so, the last time he'd passed her the flask, it had felt alarmingly light. She felt as if they'd been trekking for days, yet the sun was still only a quarter of the way up. The air had grown hotter with frightening speed. Salome's tongue felt thick in her mouth, her mouth seemed like it was lined with sandpaper, and she had a feeling she'd never get rid of the gritty grains of sand between her teeth.

Yet another dune rose before them, almost impossibly steep, and Akane groaned in dismay. "I know about false summits," she rasped. "But this beats all. Slack, are you sure this is the right way?"

"I'm sure of it." His voice was hoarse. "But I don't know the exact location of the Scarab's Temple. It won't be in sight by the time we've reached to the coordinates I'm looking for."

John scrambled up the slope, his boots sliding in the soft sand. "We'll find it somehow. We have to. It's getting hotter."

Exhausted, Salome struggled up the dune behind him. As he reached the crest, John halted, swaying slightly and gasping for air. He had a T-shirt wrapped around his head, but his face was red, and his nose was already peeling.

<123>

"John, put more sunscreen on," panted Salome. "Even I'm getting sunburned."

"I can't be . . . bothered." He sank to his knees.

Salome rummaged in his pack, but her effort was unexpectedly draining. She yanked out the tube of sunscreen and squirted some on his face.

John managed a feeble laugh as he spread it around with his palms. "Salome," he murmured hoarsely, "I don't know if we're going to make it."

"We'll make it," she reassured him, a little too brightly. "We have to. We're the Ghost Network, remember?"

"We need help." With aching slowness, he pulled the water bottle from the loop on his belt. He handed it to her.

Salome unscrewed the top with a sense of dread. Peering in, she swirled the remaining water. It barely covered the bottom.

"We might be nearly at Slack's coordinates," rasped John, "but I don't think we'll get any farther."

"I've changed my mind. We need help." Salome stared at the water bottle, then held it up to show him. "Or, John? We're going to die."

"Maybe we will." John sounded alarmingly listless, and he shrugged weakly. "Where would we get help?"

Staggering to her feet, Salome stared around at the dunes. Her heart was suddenly in her throat and beating hard with fear; there was still no sign of civilization. No paved roads, no towns, as far as the eye could see. "I don't know. Oh, John, we're in deep." Her voice almost broke, and she cleared her throat, trying to summon her courage. "Can IIDA help?"

<124>

"Unless IIDA has a water tanker in the vicinity, I don't see—"
John stopped. He narrowed his eyes.

"What is it?" she asked.

"Sh." He shut his eyes tight.

Breathlessly, Salome watched him. He was silent for a long
time. At last she could bear the suspense no longer. "What are
you doing?"

"Messaging," he muttered. "Phoneless messaging."

"Messaging whom?" Salome's eyes widened.

"The nearest people." His voice was barely a scratchy whisper.
"I think I can—leave a voicemail. So to speak. I can try."

Akane at last reached the ridge, dragging Slack behind her
by the arm. "Where to now, Slack?" she urged him. "Where to?
Slack. Which direction?"

He managed a feeble nod toward the northeast. The dunes
still looked endless in every direction, and Salome's heart
plummeted in despair.

Then she squinted. Shading her eyes against the now-intense
glare of the sun, she peered into the gap between two low dunes.
Shadows moved there, and they were drawing closer.

"Horses," she whispered. "Come on!"

Shouldering her pack, she plunged down the dune toward the
cloud of dust that accompanied the horses. *Horses with riders*, she
realized with a desperate surge of hope.

Even Slack seemed to gain a new burst of energy. He
stumbled down the slope after the others and reached them
just as they were surrounded by men on horseback, their heads
swathed in thick veils, their eyes burning with hostile curiosity.

<125>

Their leader barked a volley of words that were completely incomprehensible.

Bewildered, Salome turned a circle, gaping at the horsemen. The four Ghosts pressed instinctively closer together.

"You called someone, somehow," she murmured to John. "But right now I'm not sure it helps . . . What are they saying?"

John shook his head helplessly.

She'd seen it happen to each of the others; now, suddenly, Salome saw her own vision blur, and her world became unfocused. The angry shouts of the horseman faded, and something kicked in her brain: an impulse, a command. *Something.*

And she knew what the leader was saying.

Painful as it was for her cracked lips, Salome could not help but form a broad grin. Without even thinking, she gave the leader her reply. And then the conversation was on: fluent, quick, urgent. Gradually, the leader's tone became less angry, and, suddenly, he laughed. The other three Ghosts stared at Salome in disbelief.

"Who are they?" asked John hoarsely.

She turned to them. "They're the free people. Amazigh!"

"What?" said Slack dully. He was almost on the point of collapse.

"Berbers," croaked Salome. "They were working nearby, and Aksil here was not impressed to hear a voice in his head. In fact, he was confused and pretty angry. But he understands now. And the best part?

"He's willing to help us!"

<126>

<<>>

It wasn't just directions to the Scarab's Temple that Aksil was willing to provide; it was water and a horseback trek with himself and three of his fellow herders. When he waved goodbye to them, still grinning with amusement at the witch-boy, John, who needed no iPhone, the Temple was visible in the hazy distance, and Salome knew they were rehydrated enough to make the final stretch alone.

"His name means 'cheetah,'" she told the others cheerfully, as she raised her hand in farewell to the receding dust cloud that almost obscured Aksil and his colleagues. "And he was fast, all right. I don't know what we'd have done if they hadn't come along."

"They saved our lives," said John bluntly. "And so did you, Salome. You can speak any language, huh?"

"Not anymore." She marched at his side, filled with a new energy. "I couldn't speak Berber now if you paid me a million dollars. IIDA again." She grinned. "And I guess you can communicate telepathically. *That's* handy."

He nodded, smiling. "And Slack can navigate—not just without a map but without any visible stars. And Akane can access information by meditating."

"I guess we found out more of our abilities," grinned Akane, stumbling up beside them. Slack was right behind her, sunburned but recovered. "That's what we were supposed to do here, I suppose. But I don't like their methods."

Salome felt the optimism drain out of her. "I'm looking forward to getting back to the Center," she muttered, "but not to seeing those sadists. How could they put us through all that?"

<127>

"I hope they feel guilty," rasped Akane. "*If* this was deliberate. Are we sure it was?"

"Oh, we're sure," said John grimly. "That campsite wasn't attacked. It was deliberately abandoned. Let's not kid ourselves."

Salome glanced at him, worried, but said nothing. There was no way of knowing whether Mikael had approved these training methods, but he'd certainly handpicked the staff. And John was nursing enough resentment at his father before this.

Their suspicions were confirmed as they approached the courtyard of the Temple. Salome tried to feel relief and triumph as a figure strode from the wide-open double doors toward them, but all she could feel was a burning resentment.

Youssef's dark eyes were alight with a rather sadistic delight. "Welcome back, you four," he declared, halting with his hands clasped behind his back. "And congratulations on passing your first test!"

They silently stared at him. He didn't even avert his eyes.

"Test," echoed John bitterly under his breath. "We could have died."

"*First* test?" Akane spoke more loudly and clearly, and she sounded wary.

"Yes. The first of many." Youssef grinned. "And now you're ready to start your real training: to plan a strategy and carry it out."

"Strategy for what?" asked Salome.

"To outwit and defeat your enemies, of course." Youssef was intent again, and he ignored their hostile glares. But a smirk twitched at the corner of his mouth. "Take them down. After all, it's what you're for."

<128>

Seventeen

"I get that we're training to defeat 'our enemies,'"
said Slack, twirling a pen between his fingers. "But *it's what we're
for?* We're just machines, then. No wonder they're so casual about
putting us in danger."

John glared mutinously at Slack's twirling pen. He hadn't said
much since Youssef's airily dismissive welcome home. In fact, the
Ghosts had all found themselves resentful and sour, and they'd
headed for their pods with barely a word to the teacher.

Now, the following day, they sat together at a wooden table
in the dining hall, dusty light streaming down from the high
windows. All the other students had long since left to attend
afternoon sports activities, but the Ghost Network had quietly
agreed to skip out and hope their absence wasn't noticed. There
was far too much to discuss.

Besides, not one of them felt guilty about skipping activities,
not after that crazy desert adventure. Slack's nose was still badly
burned and peeling.

"What if," said Akane slowly, "what if we could start to do something about Lykos *before* this Center decides to get us all killed?"

"Killed—and just in training," added Salome.

"I didn't like the way Youssef said 'start our real training.' First off, how could it get any more real?" Slack narrowed his eyes. "And, Salome, I know you're not sure about Salif, but Youssef has been acting a bit weird."

Akane shrugged. "He was never especially nice as a teacher, but you know he's always been fierce. He's just gotten more so since yesterday. Since we got back from the desert."

"I guess everything's just getting more serious the longer we're here," said Salome morosely. "It's just the way he is. Super-intense."

"He doesn't let up about training, does he?" Slack shrugged. "And, anyway, how long is that real training going to take? I'm not happy waiting for us to become super-cyber-soldiers or whatever, never mind dying in the process. There has to be a way we can get to Lykos before then."

"Lykos is superpowerful," mused Akane. "It's not something to be tried lightly. We *have* to be ready. There aren't any shortcuts."

"Yes, but *why* is he superpowerful?" said John, suddenly seeming to wake up. "It's not the computer skills, is it? Those are stratospheric, obviously, but they're not what makes him untouchable. It's his contacts."

"Exactly," agreed Salome. "His reputation, his name, his friends in high places. If you ask me, that's the place to hit him hardest. Are you feeling OK, John?"

<130>

"Angry, but OK." Hitching himself up to sit on the tabletop, John swung his legs thoughtfully. "You don't necessarily need hacking powers to take someone down. The Dark Web can take care of that. The information could be disseminated so fast he wouldn't have a chance of damming every leak."

"Lykos probably has tentacles all over the Dark Web, though. He'd be onto us fast." Salome tapped her nails. "Maybe faster than we can elude him, and that could be dangerous. Fatal, even."

"The same goes for the mainstream media, of course," said Slack, "unless you happened to get the right—oh!"

"The right person!" exclaimed Akane, standing up and clattering her chair back. "Guys, we *know* the right person. We've already dealt with her!"

"Sarah Lopez." Salome slapped her hand triumphantly on the table.

"She was over the moon with that scoop about the oil fields in Canada," agreed John slowly. "I think she's exactly the person to jump at this. *If* we can get the documented information to her."

Everyone fell silent. They looked at one another.

"Do we *have* documented information?" asked Slack.

"We're the Ghost Network," scoffed Akane. "If we can't get documented information, who can?"

"I know where it is," said Salome confidently. "Or at least, I know how to find out where it is. Between getting suspicious about Lykos and leaving the Wolf's Den, I watched him a *lot*. I'm pretty familiar with his cyber routines. I think this is really possible. And if we get the proof, we can upload it to IIDA, and she can take care of the rest."

<131>

"You," said Akane, "are a star, Salome. If you can find a paper trail, you might just save all our lives."

<<>>

"You get me an electronic trail," said Sarah Lopez, her voice tinny and jumpy over the weak Skype connection, "and I'll publish it."

The Ghosts clustered around John's laptop in a corner of the basement and gazed eagerly at Sarah's face. John couldn't help thinking that she did not look nearly so ecstatic as she had when they delivered di Lucci to her.

"We need time," Salome told the journalist, leaning in to the screen. "But I know we can get you undisputable proof. I promise."

"We just have to be really careful how we hack his records," added Akane. "You can imagine. We can't be noticed. But we think we know how we can do it."

Sarah was silent for so long that John was afraid the connection had broken and the screen had frozen. The signal from the hot spot on his phone was weak down here, and there was a lot of interference from the exascale computers, where programs ran constantly in the background. And if Salif walked in here on his rounds, John was pretty sure they'd all be reported instantly to Marguerite and Youssef. He glanced nervously over his shoulder.

"Listen, you guys," said Sarah at last. She heaved a sigh. "You got me solid information before. But I have to stress—you get anything on Lykos, it has to be watertight. He's powerful like you wouldn't believe."

"Oh, we don't just believe it," growled Slack. "We know it."

"You made my career," said Sarah, her dark eyes intent. "You can kill it stone dead, right before you put me in jail."

Salome clasped her hands; John noticed her knuckles were white. "We'll get you proof; we promise. Really soon."

"You do that, and you'll get your publicity," said Sarah. Her fingers strayed toward her own keyboard, but she furrowed her brow in a final warning.

"Watertight. Remember."

And the screen went dark.

Salome pushed her chair away from the desk.

Her eyes glittered as she turned to the others. "Let's go," she growled. "We can't be found down here. Look normal. Akane, you could go and find Luna. I'll take some books to the courtyard and read. John, Slack? You take the first shift. Go play *Call of Duty* or whatever it is you do. Or pretend to."

Slack grinned and saluted. "We're on it."

"We need to do it slowly," warned John. "We don't want to spark any suspicions from Lykos's web monitors. No big downloads, no huge info dump to Sarah. A trickle. She wants reliability more than speed."

"We'll work in rotation." Salome grinned. "Get going on your best-ever hacking, guys. Because speaking of watertight—we might just destroy Lykos without having to die of thirst in the desert."

<133>

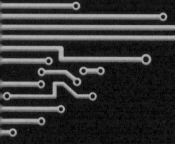

Eighteen

He had a reputation for patience. Not always with employees—he was, after all, the high-energy head of a global company, and flares of temper were to be expected from the gods of business. But trade journals and celebrity magazines alike had made it clear in multiple interviews and profiles: when he knew his target and he had no intention of missing it, Roy Lykos was a man of infinite, steely patience.

"It's time, Yasuo." Roy swung around in his chair and stared intently at his colleague.

"You're sure?"

Yasuo's question seemed merely a matter of form, so Roy didn't berate him for it. Of course he was sure; he wouldn't have bothered to say it otherwise. Yasuo knew that.

"They're still in their safe place." Roy's mouth quirked. "I like that our Ghosts feel such a sense of security. I like that they are so pleasingly complacent. And I knew, of course, that they wouldn't move. Whoever is protecting them has a little too much confidence in their abilities."

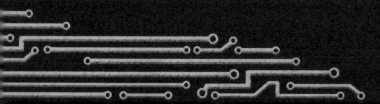

Smiling gently, Yasuo nodded. "And now you have someone in place with them. If any problems arise, you'll be notified immediately."

"And no problems have arisen so far. Just as I always expected." Roy allowed himself a quiet sigh of contentment. "The operation itself should be smooth and rapid. Of course, my traveling companion will have to be ready to accompany me."

Yasuo grinned. "She may object."

"She can object all she likes." Roy felt a twinge of dislike at the mere thought of the girl. "Make sure Miss Vygotsky is in lockdown when we're ready to move. She simply won't have time to protest."

"Consider it done." Yasuo nodded again. "All the aircraft are on standby."

"Good." Roy rose to his feet and stretched, taking a deep, satisfied breath. "As for the Ghosts, they're not going anywhere now. Not even if their protector gets nervous."

"I must say, Yasuo, I'm so looking forward to saying hello to them again."

Between the trauma of their desert trek the previous day and the excitement of *almost* dying, it was impossible to sleep. Akane clambered up the moldings on the corner of the Temple wall, hand over hand. Salif might be around, but she'd timed his patrol circuits meticulously, and right now he should be checking the vehicles in the huge garage block behind the main building.

<135>

She had time to maneuver her way over the jutting, elaborately carved cornice at the very top of the Temple.

Hanging by one hand on a molding, Akane eyed the cornice. She was familiar with its handholds now: which ones were solid and safe, which could have used a little more strengthening when they were hastily created. But the carvings and the ornamental tiling were so delicate, so elegantly formed, she did not want to snap anything off by mistake. They might not be genuinely antique, but they were beautiful, and a lot of care had gone into creating them.

Besides, much as she liked Salif, she didn't want to alert anyone on the staff. John was right: *Trust no one.* She had to do this right the first time.

Narrowing her eyes, Akane took a deep breath and jumped, high and backward. Snatching at the parapet, she found purchase and let her legs swing loose. She grabbed at the moldings with her other hand, then swung herself up and over the cornice.

Landing in a crouch, breathing hard, she stood up and stared at the Moroccan night. The sky was a deep navy; thousands of stars were still visible despite the coming dawn. There was no moon, but floodlights made pools of artificial light shimmer far below her in the courtyard. Salif stepped into one of them, peering suspiciously around, and Akane held her breath.

Salif moved on, checking alcoves in the cloister with his flashlight until he vanished around another corner.

Akane let out a sigh. Light-footed, she ran silently across the roof and scrambled up to the very highest point, an elaborately carved dome. She sat down with her back to its finial and tilted her head back to stare at the night.

<136>

It was so peaceful up here that it was almost possible to forget the endless tension of the past few days. The Ghosts had hacked, filed, downloaded, and analyzed, all while dodging Lykos's digital trip wires. Salome had been almost spot-on with her instincts; they'd found what they needed in the places she'd suggested, and when they hadn't, it had been little trouble to jump sideways or take a turn by instinct. Bit by bit, the story of Lykos's villainy was jigsawing together.

No wonder she couldn't sleep, Akane thought. She might be exhausted, but the prospect of defeating Lykos—and soon— made the blood buzz in her veins. How excited would Mikael be if they took Lykos down *before* their training was complete? And it would be one in the eye for Youssef, she thought mischievously.

Akane badly needed to meditate, to pacify and settle her racing mind. It was almost morning, and the sky would soon be pale. Taking a deep breath of the scented dawn air, Akane focused on a single brilliant star.

Slack would know its name . . .

No. Slack was a distraction. She frowned, relaxed her muscles, and tried again.

And she could have entranced herself in moments, she knew—if that star hadn't moved.

Half rising, Akane stared at it. The light was too steady to be a star; it didn't twinkle. There were more of the steadily moving lights, high above ground and away to the west. Akane glanced eastward. A pale purplish light was spreading from that horizon, the hint of a golden glow behind it, and the stars above her were beginning to fade.

<137>

Not these steady lights, though. They drew closer and closer, and Akane saw shadows become clear around them, increasingly distinct against the lightening sky.

And, suddenly, they were coming in waves. They rose over the horizon in a swarm and loomed closer by the second. They weren't birds. They were shapes she recognized, square and spidery. Akane leaped to her feet.

No!

She slithered down the dome's arch to the main roof, then ran for the cornice and threw herself over it, snatching carelessly for handholds. Her heart pulsated, and her breathing was rapid. She had to get to the others, to warn them—

The ground was not far away now. Akane released her grip and dropped lightly down to the courtyard. Glancing up, she saw the spidery shapes aligning into ranks, assembling over the courtyard like well-drilled fighter planes. Red lights blinked like malevolent eyes.

Salif, rounding the corner, stared at her in bewilderment. "Akane Maezono! What are you doing out of your room? Stop right there!"

Akane ignored him. She shouldered past him, ducking and dodging his clutching hand as he cursed. Using a burst of speed that left him grunting in shock, she raced toward her friends' quarters.

She barged into John and Slack's room without knocking. Jolted out of their sleep, they stared at her in fuzzy confusion.

"Drones!" she yelled at their stupefied faces. *"Drones are coming!"*

<138>

Nineteen

John was out of his bed and across the room, grabbing
his pack, before Akane had darted out the door to alert Salome.
Flinging T-shirts and underwear aside, he dug frantically into
the pack's depths, grabbing at solid objects. Spare toothpaste, a
camera, adaptors: he tossed them aside. Then, at last, his fingers
closed on a familiar plastic block.

He tugged it out and stared at it. The pager Mikael had given
him. If ever there was a time to use it, this had to be it.

"John Laine! Jake Hook! Akane Maezono! Salome Abraham!"

John's head jerked up, and Slack dashed toward the door and
peered out into the corridor. He turned, his eyes wide.

"It's Youssef," he hissed.

"Come into the courtyard immediately," called Youssef in a
ringing voice of command.

"What for?" whispered Slack. "An early morning workout?
What's going on?"

"I don't know. I don't like the tone of his voice." John found his
hands trembling.

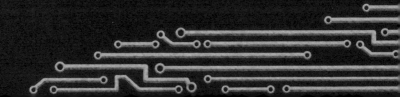

"I have no idea what's going on," said Slack grimly. "But you heard what Akane just said: drones are approaching. Something is terribly wrong."

"We have to get out of here," said John, his eyes scanning the room in a panic. But before he could even form a thought, Youssef slammed open the door, and Slack jumped back in shock.

"Didn't you hear me call you?" Youssef's eyes were steely, and John's heart plummeted. "Assemble in the courtyard now, please."

"Just us?" asked Slack suspiciously.

"Just you four," confirmed Youssef. "Though I do believe your friend Ms. Maezono has woken the entire school."

Sure enough, there was a hubbub of excited chatter as Slack and John trooped after Youssef toward the iron courtyard entrance gate. Students poked their heads around their doors, rubbing sleep-filled eyes and whispering to one another in confusion and fascination.

"This has nothing to do with you," snapped Youssef as he strode past, pulling doors shut fast enough to nip fingers. "Go back to sleep. It's not reveille time yet. Go back to your room, Luna; this is none of your business. Akane! Salome! Don't even think about sneaking off. Come with me."

But there was no stifling the curiosity of Center students, thought John wryly. As the four Ghosts were marched into the courtyard, a crowd was already assembling in the arched cloisters and staring at Youssef and his four charges.

"Look," whispered Akane to John, and pointed upward.

The drones were clearly visible now, hovering just a few feet above their heads, stacked one above the other in a hexagonal formation that covered all angles.

<140>

"We're surrounded," John murmured back to her. "Surrounded by stupid robots. What is going on?"

"Is it another test?" Akane frowned.

"Maybe," said John uncertainly. If it was, he wished the Center would quit playing with them like this. *We're not idiots!*

"I hate to suggest this," murmured Salome, "and I'm probably wrong, but what if it's not a test?"

That convinced him. *I'm sick of Youssef's games, of everybody's,* thought John. If this was another ridiculous test, he was putting in a complaint right now to the patron.

Eyeing the drones, trying hopelessly to keep track of all of them, John fumbled for the pager in his pocket. Edging behind Slack to get out of Youssef's sight line, he peered down at it. He hadn't given it much thought in the past several weeks; he'd been lulled into a false sense of safety, he thought. But the pager couldn't be hard to operate. He pressed the on button and saw the green panel glow dully.

John glanced back at the drones, fumbling to keep the pager hidden in his palm. He looked back at it, thumbed a few buttons. **I th SSsAf, DDa.** The keys were stiff and awkward, nothing like a modern touchscreen. At last, he had to peer down to hit the right letters. **D Dad. Dont know bu t I thnk We maybee R in troubl**—there was no more time. His thumb clicked on the send button—the light beam was so fast that he never saw it coming. As it struck the pager, John yelped and lost his grip. With a *pop* it tumbled to the ground at his feet, smoking, the screen dead. John stared at it in disbelief, then up at the drones, one of which was hovering elegantly back into formation with the others.

<141>

The pager was gone. His only means of contacting Mikael was now a hunk of useless plastic. John was equally terrified and furious at the same time.

"Don't move," he said angrily to the others, his eyes fixed in loathing on Youssef. "Whatever those drones are, they're not delivering from Amazon."

Salome wiped her hand across her forehead. "It's getting hot already. Youssef. Let us move to the shade."

"Stay where you are." Youssef paced back and forth in front of them. "The heat won't kill you. The drones might. Now listen carefully." He glared at his unwanted audience of students, but they were clearly going nowhere; they all watched the scene in slack-jawed amazement.

Youssef shrugged. "Salome, Akane, John, and Jake: a new security detail will shortly arrive by convoy. You will follow these men's instructions, no questions asked. Do what you're told and there won't be any consequences."

The Ghosts exchanged glances as Youssef turned away to eye the rest of the students. If this was a test, it was a pretty unsettling one.

"I told you to stay in your rooms." Youssef glared at the gathered students. "But since you're here anyway, I may as well take this opportunity to tell you. You will soon have a new headmaster." He folded his arms. "As you're aware, the Scarab's Temple has been without a principal since its recent foundation. It would have been an insult to all of you to put the wrong person in place, but the ideal candidate has finally agreed to take the position." Glancing back at John, he smiled slightly.

<142>

For just a moment, John's hope surged. This was all some annoying prank of his father's, then: a "test" of his own devising? So Mikael was finally going to show his face at the Scarab's Temple?

Then, from the crowd of watchers, Collins shouted, "Who's the new principal?"

"You may not have heard of him," grinned Youssef, his eyes twinkling with genuine excitement. "An obscure computing genius. I believe his name is . . . Roy Lykos."

<143>

Twenty

"**Did you hear that?**" said Salome bitterly. "**I thought** the Scarab's Temple student body was smarter than that. They couldn't contain themselves."

The whole courtyard had erupted at the mention of Lykos's name. Squeals of delight, shouts of disbelief. Only the four Ghosts had stood silent, numb, and shocked. The students had quickly reached a fevered pitch of happy excitement. John knew with a heavy heart that nobody really cared anymore what the four of them had done to merit being marched out of bed to the courtyard in the middle of the night. For their fellow students, there was too much else to think about. The Ghost Network, he thought dully, was on their own.

And he'd lost his dad's pager. How stupid could he have been? He didn't even know whether his desperate, barely literate message had sent.

The four Ghosts sat in Youssef's office, waiting for what felt like a sentence of execution. Youssef himself was absorbed in his laptop at his desk, ignoring them despite Salome's bitter outburst. After a long while, he closed his laptop and glanced

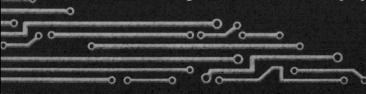

up at them. There was a cold satisfaction in his eyes, but behind it lay something else—and at last John recognized it. Only one man he knew could spark that light of fanatical devotion in his followers. *Lykos.*

"My father recruited you," John blurted out, unable to contain himself. "What happened? Why have you betrayed him?"

"It's not betrayal if you never believed in a man." Youssef pushed aside his laptop and clasped his hands on the desk. "My heart and my head have always lain with Roy Lykos. Come on, John, the man is a genius; he eclipses your father. It's like comparing the sun and the moon. Your father's plan to destroy him is a crime against technology. So, yes, I took your father's job offer. But while you were out in the desert, Roy contacted me, telling me he'd located you and asked for my help. He offered me a generous financial incentive, but I didn't even take his money. I gave him my loyalty with pride and delight. No, I'm no betrayer."

"You are," snarled John, half rising from his chair. "You're a low-down traitor. You're a snake."

Youssef shrugged and grinned. "You're quite wrong, John, and before long, you'll feel the way I do. That's inevitable, given what you are, and given Roy's eventual access to your genetic AI."

John shivered. Salome reached out and clasped his hand tightly; he could feel that she was trembling.

"None of you need to worry," Youssef went on. "As I've explained, there's nothing sinister about what has just happened. It's simply a case of a new and better school administration. But, for now, you four might find that hard to accept, and I'm sure you'll understand that I don't want you creating any discord

<145>

within the student body. Continue to study hard and obey the school rules and you'll be fine."

"We're under armed guard," snapped Slack.

"Not at all, not at all. Am I armed?" Youssef spread his arms wide. "That isn't necessary. The drones will monitor the situation constantly."

"They'll monitor *us*, you mean," muttered Akane. "That isn't sinister at all."

"You of all people should hardly be afraid of technology." Youssef smiled indulgently at her. It was funny, thought John, how his authoritarian personality had softened so suddenly with the arrival of his new master's minions. "Now, I want you all to wait in this office. I'm going to check the new arrangements in your sleeping quarters, and then you're free to go." Rising, then pausing, he added, "Within the Scarab's Temple campus, of course."

He closed the door firmly behind him, and there was a distinct click of a lock. There was silence until his footsteps had faded down the corridor. Then Slack erupted, leaping from his chair.

"How did Lykos track us down? *How?*"

"None of us contacted the outside world," cried Akane, slamming her palm onto the desk. "What is Lykos, telepathic?"

"No," said John. "I'd know if he was." Sighing, he rubbed his hands across his head. "We're just going to have to accept it. Lykos is smarter than us. He's smarter than my father. He's outwitted us. He's won."

"He's not smarter than us." Salome's voice was so quiet that they all turned toward her, falling silent themselves.

<146>

"What?" asked Slack.

"He's not clever," said Salome tearfully. She lifted her head and gazed at them all. "It's my fault."

"*What?*" they cried in unison.

"What do you mean, Salome?" said John, leaning closer. "Of course it isn't your fault!"

"It is." She raked her fingers across her braids. "Eva came looking for us. I was desperate to talk to her. I thought . . . I thought she'd found a safe channel. And Eva left flares, in the darkest corners of the web. Or . . . I thought she did. I acknowledged them."

"You *what?*" cried John.

"I thought it was just me and Eva! I thought no one else would even look! But they can't have been Eva's flares at all. Lykos must have left them. He noticed what she was doing and tracked her." Salome buried her face in her palms. "I'm *sorry.*"

Slack stared at her, his eyes filled with disbelief. "You gave away our location?"

"Not deliberately," pleaded Salome. "I thought it was safe. I . . . I stopped when the screen blipped. I shut everything down. I thought it would be OK."

"When? When was this?" Akane stood up, her fists clenched.

"A few weeks ago . . ."

"All this time?" cried Akane. Her face was a study in betrayal. "You knew you might have given away our location, and you never even said anything?"

"I thought the threat was over," whispered Salome. "Nothing happened. I thought I'd gotten away with it."

"Well," snapped Akane bitterly, "you didn't."

<147>

"Leave her alone," said John suddenly. He grasped Salome's hand and squeezed it. "There's no point in being angry. We're supposed to take the initiative, aren't we? Salome was worried about Eva. We all are! Any of us might have done this."

"*Any of us* didn't," muttered Slack. "Salome did."

"And I'm telling you: there's no point in being angry." John glared a warning at him. "Now more than ever we have to work together. We're a *team*."

Slack and Akane subsided into silence. No one said anything for a few minutes.

"The students," said Salome at last, rubbing her eyes. "There was someone missing."

"Huh?" Slack glanced at her, clearly fighting the urge to tell her to shut up. At least, thought John, he was succeeding.

"In the courtyard," Salome rushed on, suddenly much more focused. "They were all there. Everyone was out of bed by the time the drones arrived. I was watching. I'm sure of it. All of them—except one."

John drew a sharp breath. She was right.

"Zhou," he said. "Zhou wasn't in the courtyard."

<148>

Twenty-One

"Wake up, Miss Vygotsky."

The voice was silky and soft, and Eva thought for a moment that she must still be asleep. But that was not the voice of the imagined mother she had never known, the mother who only appeared, misty and insubstantial, in her dreams.

It was the voice of Roy Lykos. And something cold and metallic was pressed to her temple.

"Come with me, Eva. Immediately."

She froze. She was fully awake now. "Why?" she managed to mutter.

"We're taking a vacation," Lykos murmured. "You've been working so hard at school, and I'm sure you've been cooped up here long enough. And let's face it. I've been working hard too."

Sitting up slowly and tentatively, Eva eyed him. The gun was still pressed to her skin, against her forehead now. It was hard to see past Roy, but she could make out another figure in the light of the open doorway.

"Don't worry, Eva," said Yasuo Yamamoto, his voice gentler than Lykos's. "I promise you'll be fine. I'm sorry this is necessary, but you'll be safely back in the Wolf's Den soon. With your friends."

Eva's heart lurched. She had only three friends in the world, or four if she counted Akane, who she'd never met; what were Lykos and Yamamoto planning for the Ghost Network?

Besides, the Wolf's Den was never going to be her idea of safety.

The two men stepped outside while Eva dressed quickly in warm clothing, so she had a few moments to gather her thoughts and her courage. Trying to gather strength for what was to come, Eva stepped outside her room. They escorted her toward the stairs that led to the Wolf's Den's glass roof. She could feel Roy's gun muzzle in the small of her back; there was no question about yelling for help; besides, who would come?

At the top of the steps, Yamamoto placed his palm against the exit door, and it slid open. He was silent, but Eva heard Lykos draw an angry breath.

Little Diomede's open plateau, usually so clear and cold with its brisk Arctic wind, was almost invisible. The whole island seemed shrouded in thick, pearly fog—so dense that Eva could barely see the outline of her feet. Big Diomede, though it lay just a few miles across the ocean and the international time line, was nowhere to be seen. They might as well have been the only living creatures in the northern hemisphere.

Eva allowed herself a small, secret smile. Clearly, Lykos had not expected this.

"What the heck?" he barked behind her. "Yasuo, do something."

<150>

"Humans can control many things," said Yamamoto mildly, "but not the weather." Lykos cursed viciously.

Out of the fog, a bulky figure loomed, so abruptly that Eva choked back a scream.

"There'll be no flying in this weather, Mr. Lykos," said the figure.

"There will be flying," gritted Lykos, "when I say there will."

"It's out of the question." The pilot sounded less respectful now. "It would be crazy. Sorry, Mr. Lykos, but I won't do it."

"Oh, you will." Lykos stepped past Eva, turning his gun on the man in front of him.

The pilot gave a shocked exclamation, but Eva was unconcerned with the argument. Only one thing mattered right now. *The gun was no longer touching her.*

It was her only chance—she knew it. With a burst of speed that sent Yamamoto tumbling back in shock, Eva bolted into the mist.

She knew this plateau well—she'd spent enough time up here, gazing at the view in solitary peace—but she could not help her surge of terror. The edge of the cliff could be a few steps away; she knew it.

But the cliff wasn't the only potential peril. The gun was far more immediate. She sprinted forward into a completely invisible world, her feet tingling with the likelihood of suddenly meeting empty air.

Calm down, she told herself. *Calm down, Eva. Tune in.*

Her head lightened even as she ran, and the terror was subsumed by a cold and precise code that seemed to fill her whole skull. *Left. No, not so much. Correct course. Now. Straight ahead.*

<151>

Helicopters might not be able to fly in this fog, but Eva Vygotsky could. She hurtled on, her breath rasping, as Lykos's screams of fury were muted by the fog behind her.

"Yasuo!" came one of his yells, quite clearly. "*Get her!*"

The ground beneath her feet sloped sharply. *It's fine. Keep going.*

Eva closed her eyes. There was no point keeping them open, and it was easier to focus this way. *Slow down. Precipitous slope.* She'd reached the cliffs on the edge of Little Diomede.

One foot slid and jerked to a stop against a stone. Panting, Eva began to lurch down the steep slope, one long, jolting step after another. She stretched out her arms to balance herself. Now she could *feel* the emptiness before her: nothing but air and the surging ocean far below.

But the drop wasn't vertical. *Calm down. Calm down.*

Pebbles and stones began to rain down from the slope above her. Lykos and Yamamoto were not moving as fast as she was—they didn't have her programming, after all—but they *were* urgently following her. She heard a yelled curse, high above and behind her, and a rain of scree pattered around her, striking the back of her head and legs. *Relax. It could have been a bullet.*

It still might be, any moment.

Eva tried to descend faster. She was sliding now, her feet going from under her, and all she could do was run, the drop jolting her knees and hips with every bounding step. Faster and faster—she was out of control now—and she realized with a shock of terror that at any moment she could tumble head over heels and plummet down the remaining drop.

<152>

Her legs jolted hard, and Eva grunted with shock. The ground had leveled out. Relief flooded through her, and despite the pain in her muscles and bones, she sprinted on once more, into the impenetrable fog.

"Stop! Right now!" The bellow behind her was clear and furious. Shutting her eyes again, Eva ran faster.

A shot rang out into the murk. Eva shrieked a sob, and at last she let herself panic for a second. Her programming could tell her that the shot had been fired into the air; it didn't feel that way, though, to Eva's vulnerable human body. Tripping on an unforeseen rock, she stumbled and fell forward.

Lashing out her arms to help brace her fall, she suddenly felt herself grabbed by two strong hands.

"No!" she yelled, furious and terrified. How had Yamamoto gotten ahead of her? "Let me go! *Let me go!*"

"Hush! Eva, hush! It's fine!"

The voice wasn't Yamamoto's, and it wasn't Lykos's either. It was deep and reassuring, and it held a tinge of an imprecise Nordic accent.

"What?" she whispered, bewildered, as her pounding heart raced into overdrive. "Who—"

The man didn't have time to reply. Running feet crunched on the snow behind her, and Eva had two simultaneous, instant thoughts.

She'd run as far as the lower helipad, the one on the jutting peninsula by Diomede City.

And her pursuers had run there too, faster than she'd thought possible. They were right behind her.

"Well, well," said Lykos's voice. "Hello, the late Mikael Laine."

<153>

Twenty-Two

[T-MINUS FORTY-EIGHT HOURS]

The two weeks following the drones' arrival had been a nightmare for the Ghosts. Each of them was followed at all times by three of the machines, hovering far enough overhead not to disturb their work, but always there, always watching. John felt as if he had a constant itch at the back of his neck. Marguerite and Salif never seemed to be around—and when they were, they did everything they could to avoid speaking to the Ghosts.

The Ghosts couldn't even conspire together; they couldn't begin to make plans for their fight back. Youssef was constantly assigning them projects that kept them apart but still under the watchful eye of the drones. If two or more of them ever had a moment to talk together, Youssef would appear, smiling and friendly, and send them off with separate workloads.

And the workloads were *intense*. Had everything been normal, John wouldn't have minded; it would all have been for the good of Mikael's ultimate mission. Now, they were putting all their efforts, all their rapidly developing skills and talents, into the service of Mikael's mortal enemy, Roy Lykos. And it sucked.

There was no room for quiet rebellion either. Youssef had had weeks to get to know them and become familiar with what they were capable of. Underperforming, shirking, making elementary mistakes: even those were not possible. Youssef was onto them immediately, and with his charming persona, full of friendly smiles, he would make the darkest of threats. *For the greater good, you kids,* he would murmur. *For the greater good. You'll see it eventually.*

Nobody is indispensable, young man. Only your programming is, and that can be downloaded if we choose the more invasive techniques.

Slack, of course, had resisted immediately. It was in his DNA—his human DNA, John thought with a wry smile. But that open rebellion had been nipped in the bud, and not by Youssef.

Slack had simply turned away from Youssef as the man handed him his instructions and had marched off in the general direction of the desert. There had been nothing subtle about it—or about the response.

The same beam that had destroyed John's pager had been deployed instantly. A drone moved silently to a point directly above Slack's head, and his beloved Lakers baseball cap had been shot off his head. It had landed in the dust, a charred and smoking ruin. And that had been the end of Slack's rebellion.

For a moment, John's fingers paused on his laptop's keyboard. He did not want to address this labyrinthine coding solution. He did not want to help Roy Lykos achieve his goal. But he didn't have a choice. He had to sit here, alone in the locked tutorial room, and finish his assignment.

<155>

John didn't think Lykos genuinely wanted to use this information he was hacking from the Chinese Ministry of National Defense . . . but nothing would surprise him anymore. The last thing he wanted was to give Lykos the keys to this missile system—and expose more of his own internal AI even as he worked, because the exercise had a sinister dual purpose. John knew very well that his every keystroke was monitored and recorded. But remembering the charred baseball cap, and Youssef's smiling menaces, John shuddered and continued his work.

There was another nagging worry in the back of his mind, almost minor compared to the daily threats: there had still been no sign of Zhou Zhou. Youssef never mentioned Zhou's absence; no one did.

Marguerite or Salif might know where the boy was, but they were silenced; either they were in cahoots with Lykos too or they were kept firmly in line by Youssef and the drones. John had locked gazes with Marguerite once or twice; she had looked tormented, but he hadn't had a chance to exchange a single word with her. Salif simply avoided his gaze.

Truthfully, John had no idea whether the two of them were in on this. He didn't *think* so, from the way Marguerite and Salif moved around campus, shoulders resentfully slumped. But he didn't *know*. Anything that happened, any action by anyone outside the Ghost Network, could be one of Lykos's ruses. Marguerite and Salif could possibly be faking their reluctance.

The Ghosts could trust only one another. No one else.

And somewhere, silent and invisible, lurked a Chinese computer genius who could make lethal bombs with nothing but his mind.

<156>

Twenty-Three

[T-MINUS TWENTY-FOUR HOURS]

In the swirling Alaskan murk, Eva gasped. She stared up at the man who clutched her arms. Graying blond hair swept back from a widow's peak, bright blue eyes that penetrated even the fog.

In fact, the fog was beginning to lift. At last Eva could see a clear circle for perhaps thirty feet around her. She shook off Mikael's grip and spun round. Lykos stood there, his gun raised, grinning.

"Hello, Roy," said Mikael.

Eva trembled. The atmosphere between the two men was so charged that she could almost feel electric sparks. The two stood and stared at each other across the flat helipad. Behind Lykos, Yamamoto and the pilot stumbled to a halt and watched the scene warily.

Gently, Mikael took Eva's arm again and drew her protectively behind him. "You can't have her, Roy," he said.

"She's mine," said Roy coldly. "She's . . . how do we say it, Mikael? My intellectual property. You relinquished your own claim when . . ." He tilted his head and examined Mikael. If he was surprised, Lykos was clearly determined to give no sign of it. "When you so obviously faked your own death. Welcome back to the world of the living, Mikael. However briefly."

Mikael watched him, saying nothing. Eva's heart felt as if it was stuck in her throat. Then, as if a command prompt had lit up on her internal screen, she remembered something.

My phone. They'd taken her SIM card, they'd disabled the Wi-Fi, but they left her useless phone. Maybe it wasn't entirely useless. She drew it cautiously from her pocket.

"That's quite a deceit you pulled, old friend," murmured Lykos.

"It was necessary," said Mikael quietly. "You made it necessary."

"I daresay I did. And congratulations on fooling me for so long. Not many can do that." Lykos's face grew hard. "I see you were reborn with superpowers, like Gandalf. How very impressive that you can swim across the Bering Strait." He looked Mikael up and down, with insulting slowness. "Without even getting your feet wet."

Mikael shrugged and gave him a slight smile. "I'm well connected in the helicopter industry."

Roy's eyes widened, the irises darkening almost to black. For the first time, he looked genuinely shocked. "Walt has been my pilot for twenty years!"

"Walt," said Mikael calmly, "has been my friend for twenty-eight."

It happened fast. As Lykos swung around to face the helicopter pilot, Walt lunged toward him, snatching at the gun. At exactly the same moment, Mikael shoved Eva hard toward the helipad.

"*Run!*" he yelled.

<158>

Eva needed no second command. She sprinted for the helicopter, now a distinct bulky shape in the lightening air. She could hear Mikael's running steps behind her and the sounds of a struggle: grunting, shouts, and blows. As she reached the chopper's skids, she swung round.

The fog had lifted, leaving a few misty wisps. She saw Lykos stumble back and heard a shot ring out. She saw Walt flung backward by the impact of a bullet. Then his body hit the tarmac with a sickening thump, and he lay sprawled, his legs jerking. In a few seconds, he went limp.

Every bone in Eva's body went cold. Her blood seemed to have slowed to a trickle in her veins. She could not take her eyes off the pilot's inert body. Her brain seemed to detach from her body, floating and wobbling, and she felt as if she might be sick. Somehow, her phone stayed clutched in her numb fingers.

"Get in!" yelled Mikael. He shoved Eva, shocked and unresisting, into the belly of the chopper. He scrambled in after her, fumbled between the pilot seats, then crouched at the hatch, firing rhythmically and widely across the apron of ground between him and Lykos.

"Hold it," he commanded, pushing the gun into Eva's trembling hands as Lykos and Yamamoto dived for cover. "You don't have to shoot anyone. Just keep firing!"

Eva nodded, her mind cooling and settling. *I'm Eva Vygotsky,* she told herself harshly. *I don't do shocked damsel. Do what has to be done. Then think about that poor pilot.*

Doing as Mikael asked, Eva squeezed the trigger, firing steadily across the peninsula as Mikael scrambled into the pilot seat. The rotors slowly spun into action, she heard the engine

<159>

rumble, and then the whole helicopter gave a jolt that made her grab for the edge of the hatch.

"Hold on," shouted Mikael over the noise of the rotors.

Eva crouched against the hatch, gripping it for her dear life, as the helicopter rose slowly into the air. She couldn't even hold the gun now, let alone fire it, and Lykos and Yamamoto were getting to their feet, running once more toward the chopper. "The fog?" she shouted.

"We'll be fine." Mikael swung the aircraft round. Eva swayed and gripped the hatch harder. "Get inside," he added. "Don't fall out now, kid, whatever you do."

"I won't." But Eva was grinning now, as she clambered to the other seat and grabbed for the seat belt. Lykos continued firing, but the sound of his shots was already distant. In what seemed like just a matter of moments, Little Diomede was far below and behind them.

Eva closed her eyes and breathed deeply, then blinked them open. She could already make out the Alaska coastline, between the gray sky and the heaving, metallic sea.

"I'm sorry," she said, as shock returned to hit her once again. "The pilot. Walt. Oh God, I'm sorry."

Mikael swallowed hard and shook his head grimly. "So am I. But Walt attacked Lykos because he wanted to give you a chance. I couldn't waste it. I just wish I could be certain Lykos will pay for that, but the first thing he'll do is get rid of Walt's body. And we'll have no proof he fired that shot at all."

Eva smiled and was silent for a long time until, finally, Mikael turned to eye her quizzically. She lifted her phone and turned its screen toward him.

<160>

"Yes, we do," she told him. "Say the word and all of Snapchat will have the proof."

Mikael gave a wild growl of triumph and took his hand off the steering column long enough to give Eva an almost violent high five. "You *star*, Eva Vygotsky. Leave Snapchat for now. Just watch that video through, access your programming, and you'll be able to upload it to your own brain. IIDA will do the rest. She's a whole lot more efficient than the Cloud—you have my word on it." He chuckled darkly.

"Salome and the others," said Eva suddenly, her high mood slightly dampening. "John, Slack, and Akane. I don't know what's happening to them. I know where they are, and I saw their location—but *so did Lykos*."

"Don't worry. Not yet, anyway. I think they're safe for now, Eva." There was solid land beneath them, so Mikael began to angle the helicopter into a descent toward Wales Airport. "Why do you think I didn't confront Roy on the upper helipad? Walt bought me time to break into the Center and access Project 31. I know the access codes by heart, and Lykos hadn't changed them; why would he? He thought I was dead."

Hope rose in Eva again. "So what did you do?"

He shrugged. "Just a temporary fix. But I activated the mainframe and overrode every one of Roy's commands that I could find. It was the first thing I had to do. I'm sorry I couldn't come to you first, Eva."

"That's OK. If it helped the others, I'm glad. Even if that run across the island *was* the most terrifying thing I've ever done." She grinned.

<161>

Mikael nodded as he set the helicopter jerkily down on the Wales helipad. "I've bought the Ghosts some time, Eva. Now I need to contact John. And at last I can do that, through you. The programming is available. I know because I put it there, a long time ago. I would have to wait; I can't do it yet. The timing's important." He raised his eyebrows, suddenly questioning. "But, much more importantly, I don't want to invade your mind without permission. I won't."

Eva turned in her seat and smiled at him.

"It's about time, Mister Mikael Laine. Be my guest."

<162>

Twenty-Four

[T-MINUS TEN MINUTES]

John jolted forward in his seat, bumping his stomach on the desk. He shook his head.

Youssef was on the podium in front of his whiteboard when he looked sharply at him. "John. Is something wrong?"

John shook his head again hard, this time at Youssef. He forced a smile through the sudden headache.

"No. Thought I saw a scorpion. Sorry."

With a roll of his eyes, Youssef smirked. "Very well. Since class is almost over, I'll allow the distraction, just this once. But you'll have to be tougher than that, Mr. Laine. Scorpions are the least of your worries in the career you're preparing for."

John suppressed a shiver and nodded coldly at Youssef. As the teacher turned back to his laptop, Akane leaned over from the next desk and whispered urgently.

"Something *is* wrong. What is it?"

John shot her a warning glance. "Later," he mouthed.

Six minutes later, they had packed up their laptops and were heading out to the courtyard for a break, followed all the time by

Youssef's glittering, intense gaze. John scratched the back of his neck, stepped into the sunlit courtyard, and nodded to Slack and Salome. They came hurrying over to join him and Akane.

"Something's up," Akane told them in a murmur before John could speak. She flicked her eyes toward the sky.

Their unwanted monitors were still there. Sun glinted off the white metal of the drones. They hovered, still and menacing, some one hundred feet above the Ghosts' heads.

"Stupid things," muttered Slack. "So tell us, John."

"I don't know what to tell you." He shrugged helplessly. "I had a sudden command prompt. Inside, I mean."

"Telepathy again?" asked Salome nervously. "Whose?"

"What passes for telepathy in my programming," John corrected her. "And I honestly have no idea who it was." He glanced around, checking for intruders other than the drones. "It was kind of a . . . a holding command, that's all. *Wait . . . command incoming.* Like that, sort of."

"But why now—" began Slack, but he was cut off by John's strangled cry of shock.

John could just make out his friends' faces, but they were fading. No, not fading—but it was as if a window had been minimized. They were speaking to him, urgently, quietly, and distantly. He could feel Slack shaking his shoulder, but their voices had been muted into silence.

The prompts came thick and fast, pouring into his brain, but one command glared out from the rest, distinct and loud, impossible to ignore.

Run!

John clutched at his head. *I can't. I can't. They'll shoot me.*

<164>

No. They won't. RUN.

Three drones are on me! Monitoring every step! I can't.

Leap of faith, John. LEAP OF FAITH. They will not fire. RUN.

John could not move. He knew he was shaking, but he couldn't stop it, and he couldn't respond to his increasingly fearful friends who now crowded around him. The fact was he was scared; he was too scared to run. He didn't even know who this was. It could be Lykos, trying to kill him. It could be Youssef, playing a vicious trick to test his rebelliousness. *He could die.*

John. John. Trust me. You are the computer, John. Remember? Now, run.

John clenched his teeth. *Dad? Dad?*

You have my word. Help is coming, but you have to go NOW. Trust me. RUN.

The programming faded. His brain was back—the part of his brain he'd been born with, anyway. John straightened, pushing Slack and Salome away. His face set hard.

"Run!" he barked, bolting for the courtyard gateway.

The others didn't ask questions; maybe it was their own programming, or maybe they had all been together long enough now. They had to trust him completely. He could hear all three of his friends behind him, their feet pounding hard on compacted sand. They burst through the gateway, John in the lead, and simply ran, straight toward the desert.

"Hey! Get back! Get *back!*" Youssef's furious, shocked yell echoed behind them, but they didn't slacken their pace.

All your punishment running circuits, Youssef, you jerk, thought John bitterly as he sprinted. *They came in more useful than even you expected.*

<165>

But what was the point of this sudden, frantic escape? *Trust me*, the programming had said. Where was John running to, and what was waiting for them?

It didn't matter. All they could do now was keep running.

Youssef, too, was running. He wasn't shouting anymore; when John risked a glance over his shoulder, he saw the man sprinting after them, his face grim and determined. Lykos's henchmen were racing after him too, responding to Youssef's summons.

But John saw something else too: students pouring from the Temple. They were fleeing as if their lives depended on it, tumbling out of doorways, crowding and shoving through the courtyard gateway, dropping the short distance from first-level classrooms. John caught sight of Salif, catching a couple of smaller boys and then running with them, shepherding them away from the Temple.

He couldn't watch anymore. Youssef was drawing closer to him and his friends. John faced forward again and put forth another burst of speed.

And then he saw a figure. Slim and tall, a boy stood facing him some thirty yards away. He looked perfectly calm and still, and he held something compact and square in his hand. John had not seen the boy for weeks, but he knew him.

Zhou!

John's heart lurched. Was it an ambush? Was Zhou with Youssef? There was no way of knowing, but the command was hardwired in John's head. He had to keep running, he had to—

Zhou remained perfectly motionless as John pounded across the sand toward him. Then, with the slightest of motions, Zhou's thumb twitched on the thing in his hand.

<166>

The blast wave caught John in the small of the back, driving him forward and sending him crashing onto his face in the sand. Only then did he hear the explosion, and when he caught his breath and crawled onto his hands and knees, he looked back to see the Scarab's Temple evaporate in a ball of flame.

The sound of crashing stone and collapsing towers was deafening, or maybe the blast had ruptured his eardrums. John gaped, stunned, as the ball of flame subsided and the Temple crashed down into a ruin of rubble. A column of black smoke was all that remained, climbing toward the blue desert sky.

Gasping for breath and winded, John staggered to his feet. He hauled Salome up and noticed Akane helping Slack. But not far behind them, Youssef, too, was clambering upright, his face murderous.

The drones. I haven't had time to think about it. The drones didn't fire on us. And Youssef doesn't know why.

"Run!" John shouted again, and they all staggered back into a stumbling jog.

"We're not going to outrun him," panted Salome, glancing back. "He's still coming!"

A huge fan of sand sprayed up, off to their left-hand side, and a startled John glanced to the side. A dune buggy screamed to a halt beside them, and John felt his nerves spark into readiness for a fight.

But it was Zhou Zhou who leaped up from behind the wheel. "Get in. Get in!"

They needed no more instruction. Akane leaped in like a gazelle, and the others scrambled after her. They had barely

<167>

landed in the back when Zhou stamped on the gas and the dune buggy shot off toward the desert.

John craned his neck around. Youssef was still running, but he was slowing now, and John was relieved he couldn't hear the man's curses. All he could make out was an incomprehensible torrent of screaming, and then Youssef was lost in the clouds of sand kicked up by the dune buggy.

The woman in the front passenger seat turned to smile at them, shoving wild strands of dark hair from her eyes.

"That was close, Ghosts," grinned Marguerite Lagarde. "Welcome aboard Air Zhou Zhou!"

<168>

Twenty-Five

"Emergency exits," said Zhou dryly as Marguerite made a pantomime of gesturing all around the buggy. "Do not remove your shoes if the slides inflate."

"Funny." Slack risked punching his shoulder, and Zhou did not even retaliate.

John stared at Zhou, a little confused. Had the grim-faced boy actually made a *joke*?

Akane started to laugh, and soon all four Ghosts caught the bug, giggling helplessly with the release of tension. At last John wiped his eyes.

"But how did you know? What have you guys been up to? Zhou, where have you *been* for the past couple of weeks? Were you confined to your pod this whole time?"

Marguerite nodded at Zhou beside her. "This genius has been in contact with your dad since before the drones arrived, John. Even Roy Lykos would have trouble monitoring this one." Fondly, she tousled Zhou's black hair, and he flicked away her hand. "Salif and I were alarmed when Zhou came to the school, to say the least—what with his penchant for *destroying stuff*—but he's been working for Mikael since he hacked into the blueprints for the Ghost Network project."

"It's a good program," interjected Zhou, "but only when it's in good hands."

"The moment we realized those drones had arrived, we sneaked Zhou out of his pod and into a safe house," Marguerite went on.

"Safe what?" asked Zhou. "More like a safe cave."

"You're my new favorite person, Zhou," Salome told him warmly. "Oh and you, Marguerite. So Salif's on our side too? Will he be OK?"

"He stayed behind and started getting the students out, ahead of Mikael's counterattack," smiled Marguerite. "We knew it would be a tight timescale. It had to happen after your father regained control of the mainframe and got himself to Morocco but before Youssef was onto what was happening. But I knew I could trust Salif. There might have been some PSPs and some Xboxes among the casualties, I'm afraid, along with the Center's equipment. But no human beings."

"I saw Salif," grinned John. "He was running with the last students when the building blew. I'm sure he was far enough away—Youssef certainly was. He's fine."

Salome puffed out a sigh of happy relief.

"But the Center?" said Slack, staring back at the column of black smoke that rose beyond the dunes. "Your dad poured a lot into that place, John."

"Mikael knew that the Center was effectively burned as soon as Lykos located it," said Marguerite darkly. "He knew it was better to destroy it than see it fall into Lykos's hands. And if

<170>

this all turned out the way he hoped, he knew he'd have other options."

John narrowed his eyes. "I wonder if he half expected this to happen? The Scarab's Temple wasn't—"

"Much like the other Centers?" Marguerite gave a dry laugh. "Indeed, John. Mikael does like to try to stay a few steps ahead. I'm sure he foresaw Lykos getting to this place, and that's why he didn't exactly, uh . . . invest all his available resources." She winked. "I believe those fancy computers in the basement will be fine, if that's any comfort. Your dad was very specific about installing them below ground level. Maybe one day we can retrieve them."

"Maybe. But we're not out of the woods yet—or the desert," said Zhou, as he bumped the buggy over a ridge of hard sand. "We don't have much in the way of supplies. I took just enough to get us safely away—I didn't want to raise any suspicions."

"The important thing was to get everyone out of the Temple," Marguerite reassured him.

"We have limited water," Zhou pointed out grimly. "And, what's more, this dune buggy doesn't carry magic unlimited fuel. We've got to get a good distance into the desert, but after that, we're walking. We can rig a makeshift shelter over the buggy and sleep inside it, but food and water are going to be strictly rationed. All while avoiding Youssef."

"Not another desert trek," groaned Slack.

"So we're not out of the woods yet," said Salome. "Or even the desert."

"Does this thing go faster, Zhou?" asked Marguerite, with an anxious glance over her shoulder. "It won't take Youssef and his

<171>

men long to regroup. We have to get clear of their pursuit. After that—we'll be fine. Somehow."

John exchanged an uncertain glance with Akane, who made a face.

We only have to get clear. We'll be fine.

He was pretty sure they'd all heard that one before . . .

<<>>

The buggy bounced and veered as Zhou drove it like a maniac across the ridged sand. They clutched the sides, hearts in their mouths.

"You've been brilliant, Zhou," shouted Akane, turning to him. "Just wanted to say that, in case they catch us."

Slack had been staring nervously back toward the clouds of dust in the distance and the vague shimmering outlines of pursuing vehicles. Now he twisted and gave Zhou a sourly jealous glance.

Zhou shrugged as he drove. "I told you," he yelled. "I hacked into the Ghost Network files some months ago, when my father told me he was sending me to the Center. I found the hidden files by accident. So I made it my business to dig deeper."

"And we're glad you did. We—" Akane's smile suddenly froze. She stiffened, and her eyes grew vague and faraway.

Zhou looked at her quizzically, then turned his attention back to navigating the dunes. John, Salome, and Slack, though, stared at her. They exchanged apprehensive glances.

"Akane," said Salome gently. "What's wrong?"

Akane was silent a moment longer. Then she shook herself.

<172>

"Incoming," she gritted.

"What is?" Alarmed, John turned to scan the dunes. "The drones?"

Akane pointed upward. "No. *Plane.*"

Almost as soon as she said the words, they heard the distant hum. Far too quickly, the sound became a really loud drone, and Zhou braked hard. As the buggy jolted to a halt in the sand, sunlight glinted on something white rising over the horizon.

John stood up in the buggy, gripping the frame. In seconds the drone had become a roar, and the small plane soared close overhead, its engine deafening. John and the others ducked, shielding their heads with their arms and shutting their eyes against the rising clouds of sand.

"What the—" yelled Slack. "That is *low.*"

The plane's wheels touched down on a stretch of hard sand, digging deep into it and throwing up more choking clouds. Between them and their distant pursuers, it bumped and rolled to a halt, and the propellers slowed.

"Lykos," rasped Salome. She sounded as if she wanted to either cry or murder someone.

Marguerite stood up, scanning the dunes urgently. "Some of the dunes are high. We might be able to hide, if we can get farther," she said grimly, "but it's open here. They must have seen us, and they'll see which direction we take."

"They have a *plane*," pointed out Akane. "And it's a Twin Otter. They can take off from there, no problem."

"Smart," said Zhou with an admiring glance. "You know a lot."

"Smart programming," admitted Akane, tapping her temple.

<173>

"Never mind Akane's extensive knowledge of aircraft," put in Slack, rather sharply. "We have a problem!"

"No," said Zhou, shading his eyes to peer at the aircraft. His smile was all the more brilliant because it was so rare. "We don't."

Salome was standing up, resting one hand on the buggy frame as she shielded her eyes with the other. Suddenly, she gave a shout of delight. "It isn't Lykos!"

"Who is it, then?" Slack jumped up to peer out beside her.

"It's your dad, John!" Salome gave a whoop and punched the air. "*And Eva!*"

She was already running before John and the others were out of the buggy. Bolting across the dunes, she almost collided with the small, slight figure who was sprinting toward her. The two girls embraced and spun each other round, squealing with delight.

More sedately, a tall blond figure strode toward them, grinning. John's heart turned over with happiness and relief.

"Dad!"

He flew into his father's waiting arms, and soon the others were gathered around them, hugging and yelling with triumphant happiness.

"Who was flying?" grinned Salome. "Was it you, Eva?"

"Hey, don't joke!" Eva laughed. "I *did* fly a few of the legs!"

"And she was brilliant at it," added Mikael, his arm tight around John's shoulders. "Luckily. Because we've been plane-hopping all the way from Alaska, and I had to sleep *some* of the time!"

"I learned everything I know from Salome," smiled Eva. "Long-distance. That was quite a download!"

<174>

"And I didn't even know," laughed Salome. "But it must have been quicker than learning from scratch!"

"I wanted to contact you earlier." Mikael gripped John's shoulders, gazing into his eyes. "I got Eva away from Lykos, and I knew I could get you guys out of here, but we had to fly halfway across the world first. I had to go to Alaska to disable those drones. It was agony waiting to contact you through Eva, but I made the telepathic connection as soon as I could. We had to time it just right—the destruction of the Temple, getting you clear with the help of Marguerite, Salif, and Zhou. By the time I knew it was safe to talk to you, John, I was so desperate I may have rushed it. I hope I didn't give you a headache."

"You did," admitted John. "But it was worth it!"

"Where *is* Lykos?" asked Akane suddenly.

"In the FBI's custody," said Mikael with a triumphant grin.

"Wow." Slack stared at Mikael. "They've pinned something on Lykos? With all his high-level contacts?"

"They have." Mikael nodded. "The other charges can come later, but right now he's been arrested for murder. There isn't a senator or a police commissioner who can whitewash *that* away." His face darkened. "Roy killed a good man. And he would never have been held to account for it if Eva hadn't caught the very act on her camera phone. She's a quick thinker in a crisis."

Wryly, Eva tapped her head.

"No," insisted Mikael. "That wasn't your programming, Eva. That was all you."

Eva's usually pale and solemn face was tinged with a pink blush. "Really?"

<175>

"Really." Michael smiled at her. "We still don't know your history, Eva. But you've got one. Eva Vygotsky was there long before her programming was, and it seems she was a pretty amazing person. Still is."

Eva flung herself at Mikael and gave him an impulsive hug. Slack grinned. "Eva! You're human!"

"Of course she is," Akane scolded him with a grin. "And right now—sorry, Zhou"—she nodded at the plane, glinting in the early sun—"but Eva's my favorite human being in the world."

"Not me?" asked a deep voice. "When I knew very well you were scuttling over the roof at night and I pretended not to see you?"

When they all turned, Salif was grinning at them, the escaped students clustered behind him.

Akane squealed. "Salif! Yes! And you, Marguerite!" Impulsively, she hugged them both; Salif looked surprised but pleased. "Thank you," she murmured. "For being on our side."

"Where did Youssef go wrong?" asked Slack glumly.

"I can explain part of that," said Salif. "I've been putting out feelers about him; I never thought he was quite right. That man has a whole empire of developers working under him; he's notorious in Casablanca. He runs a Dark Web infrastructure that covers the whole North African region." He smiled and added wryly, "And he's a Roy Lykos fanboy, as we discovered too late. Youssef would do anything for that man."

"He'd even keep kids captive when he was paid to protect them," growled Marguerite angrily.

"And you guys stopped him," pointed out Akane. "You saved us from a fate worse than death. *Literally.*"

<176>

Mikael grinned. "By the way, I hope Eva's going to come back to school?" He turned and gave Eva a questioning glance. "She's as much a Ghost as the rest of you."

"Absolutely!" Salome grinned and hugged her friend.

"Of course I want to come back to school." Eva was blushing furiously now. "I'd love to."

"Um," said John, pointing back at the smoldering ruins of the Scarab's Temple. "There's just one problem with that, Dad."

"Oh, I don't mean the Scarab's Temple," said Mikael cheerfully. "That was the right place for you at the right time, but its purpose is finished. There's only one place you truly belong." Slack stared at him, and, slowly, he began to grin.

"You mean we can go back . . ."

"I mean exactly that." Mikael threw his arm around John's shoulder again. "You're going back home, guys. To the Wolf's Den!"

<177>

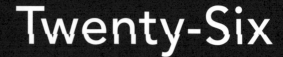

Twenty-Six

"I wish you'd come with us to Alaska, Zhou." With hastily bought clothes and belongings packed in his brand-new bag at his feet, John gazed seriously at Zhou's impassive face and held out his hand. "The Wolf's Den is . . . well, you can't believe it till you see it. You belong there, like we do." He tapped his temple and smiled wryly. "You've got the Ghost DNA too, and yours can already do incredible stuff. My dad can teach you how to channel it . . ."

A smile flickered, just briefly, at the corner of Zhou's mouth. He clasped John's hand.

"No." His tone was final. "I've learned on my own how to channel my abilities, and I think I'm doing OK."

"That's an understatement," muttered Slack.

Zhou laughed. "Goodbye, Jake Hook. It's been fun getting to know you."

"I've gotta admit, same to you." Slack gave him a wry grin and shook his hand.

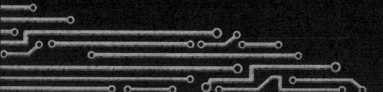

John gave his friend a sidelong glance, amused. Slack had been far more relaxed around Zhou since he had declared he wasn't coming with them to the Wolf's Den.

Slack's sudden chilled attitude had nothing to do with a certain parkour fanatic from Tokyo, of course, thought John with an inward laugh.

"There's something you don't understand," said Zhou. "I don't want you to think I'm not coming because I *think I'm better than you*, or anything." He gave Slack a knowing look. "My father worked for yours, John. I mean, in one of his labs. After my own accident, I was one of the test subjects for Phase 2."

"Ah." John stared, taken aback. "That's why you have talents way ahead of ours?"

"And more controllable ones," said Mikael, walking over from the airport security line. "Phase 2 was exciting, and it was way, way ahead of its time, John. But it got out of hand." He glanced at Zhou. "Phase 2 is when Roy and I had our fallout."

A tiny announcement rang out over the airport's PA system, and travelers around them began to rise, gather their luggage, and head for the boarding gate. The former Scarab's Temple students, Collins and Luna among them, began to drift toward the gate too, but the Ghosts lingered, reluctantly.

"You're going back to your true home," Zhou went on, "and I'm going back to mine—Chongqing. I've got a *lot* to tell my father about the school he chose for me. And the life."

"So you won't return to the Centers at all?" Salome looked dismayed.

"Oh, there's a Center in Shanghai," Zhou assured her. "That's the one I'll be attending—it's only a few hundred miles from

<179>

home instead of thousands. A pretty amazing Qing dynasty palace, by all accounts." He winked. "I won't be missing out. And we *will* see each other again. I've no doubt we'll all be in contact once we've graduated next year."

"That," said Salome, "is the best news yet." She hugged Zhou, and to the surprise of absolutely everyone, he hugged her back.

"Better news than defeating Roy Lykos?" asked Akane in amusement.

"Whoa." Mikael held up their boarding cards, fanned in his hand. "We haven't *quite* beaten him yet, my Ghosts." He grinned. "But we're well on the way."

"Oh, I have no worries on that score." Akane embraced Zhou and smiled, then picked up her pack.

"That psycho will be behind bars for a *very* long time!"

<180>

Epilogue

Carlos Sanchez Ramirez and Imogen Black beamed and
applauded from the back of the atrium. Howard McAuliffe, the
famed "Most Boring Teacher at the Wolf 's Den," was dancing
a little jig and punching the air, and he slapped Principal Reiffelt
enthusiastically on the back as she strode past him. She halted,
her face pale and stiff with the sheer shock of the affront; then
she suddenly grinned, her austere face transformed, and kissed
him neatly on both cheeks.

The student body whooped and applauded as their exiled
members stood in front of them all, blushing with embarrassment and looking agonizingly awkward: John Laine, Jake Hook,
Salome Abraham, new girl Akane Maezono, and Eva Vygotsky.
Eva was the only one of them who looked at all calm: her pale
face was serene and cool.

With them stood Mikael Laine; he was grinning as Principal
Reiffelt approached him. She embraced him formally, kissed
his cheeks, then turned to face the students. Then, shrugging,
she spun on her heel and went back to Mikael for a much more
energetic hug.

The students erupted in hoots and yells of approval—especially the newly matriculated group, who included an aristocratic Nigerian boy and a blonde Cornish girl. It took some time to calm the student body down, but Irma Reiffelt's stern ex-Stasi face eventually did the trick.

"Ladies and gentlemen, students of the Wolf's Den," she began. "It gives me more pleasure than you can imagine to introduce our new headmaster, Mikael Laine. You have all heard by now the rumors about our previous head teacher's departure and what brought it about. I'm well aware that this gossip is rife: tales of espionage, perilous risk, and desert adventures." A smile formed at the very edge of her mouth in the expectant silence. "I am here to tell you that the rumors are true . . ."

<<>>

As the laughter and cheers rose around them, Adam Kruz turned to Leo Pallikaris, his eyes glinting with furious resentment.

"I've heard enough of this garbage," he growled. "Let's get out of here."

"We'll get in trouble with Ms. Reiffelt . . ." said Leo.

"No, we won't. Everybody's busy with the Adoration of Mikael. Let's go."

Adam was right; no one noticed them go. Clenching his teeth, clutching his laptop hard against his chest, he marched up the glowing glass ramp toward Yasuo Yamamoto's old office. Adam felt bitterness seethe inside him.

<182>

"Roy Lykos was the only one who recognized our potential," he told Leo. "And you're crazy if you think I'm going to let this farce go unchallenged. He's preening up there with his ridiculous son and his friends, but Mikael Laine isn't worthy to lick Roy's boots."

"It made me sick," agreed Leo hastily.

"That's why we're going to do something about it." Adam sat down at Yasuo's old desk and opened his laptop. "The FBI thinks Roy can't get a message to me? He's a million light-years beyond their comprehension, the dullards." Leaning forward as Leo came to stand eagerly behind him, Adam woke up the screen.

Roy Lykos's narrow, intelligent face gazed out at them. It broke Adam's heart to see him handcuffed, to see this mighty genius in an orange prison jumpsuit. *How dare they.*

"Roy. They had better be treating you well." Adam glared at the shadowy figure behind his mentor. Who was that, a guard? Brutes.

Roy clasped his hands. He glanced back at the figure behind him. "Don't worry, Adam, Leo. They're treating me very well indeed. It's good to see you, boys."

Then Roy grinned and winked, and his eyes glinted.

"And, now, we're really going to get to work."

. . . Waiting for download . . .

<183>

Look for these books!

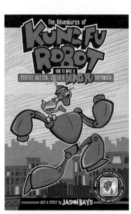

Listen up! Enjoy *The Ghost Network* series in audio, wherever audiobooks are sold.